A
CONFLAGRATION
ARTIST

A CONFLAGRATION ARTIST

BRADLEY DENTON

ILLUSTRATED BY

DOUG POTTER

THE WILDSIDE PRESS
NEWARK, NJ ○ 1993

A Conflagration Artist

And this one's for Barb, too.

An original publication of The Wildside Press. No portion of this book may be reproduced by any means, electronic or otherwise, without the express written consent of the author. For more information, contact: The Wildside Press, 37 Fillmore Street, Newark, NJ 07105.

"In the Fullness of Time" originally appeared in *The Magazine of Fantasy & Science Fiction*, May 1986. "Top of the Charts" originally appeared in *The Magazine of Fantasy & Science Fiction*, March 1985. "Killing Weeds" originally appeared in *The Magazine of Fantasy & Science Fiction*, November 1986. "The Music of the Spheres" originally appeared in *The Magazine of Fantasy & Science Fiction*, March 1984. "The Summer We Saw Diana" originally appeared in *The Magazine of Fantasy & Science Fiction*, August 1985. "Captain Coyote's Last Hunt" originally appeared in *Isaac Asimov's Science Fiction Magazine*, March 1990. "The Chaff He Will Burn" originally appeared in *The Magazine of Fantasy & Science Fiction*, April 1990. "A Conflagration Artist" appears in this collection for the first time.

Printed in the USA by Baker-Johnson Printing.

ISBN: 1-880448-40-8 (26-copy lettered hardcover edition)
ISBN: 1-880448-41-6 (100-copy numbered hardcover edition)
ISBN: 1-880448-42-4 (300-copy trade hardcover edition)
ISBN: 1-880448-90-4
FIRST EDITION: NOVEMBER 1993
November 1993

CONTENTS

INTRODUCTION

BY STEVEN GOULD

I needed a title for this introduction.

My wife, Laura J. Mixon, suggested, "Brad Denton — what a babe." I reject this without consideration.

Brad's and my mutual friend, Robin W. Bailey, suggested, "Brad Denton — what a babe." Better, but not quite there yet.

Brad's wife, Barb Denton, suggested, "Brad Denton — what a babe."

Okay, now we're getting somewhere.

Picture a man, young, blond, bearded, conservatively cut hair, glasses thick enough to stop neutrons, and a pronounced tendency to blush and stammer with embarrassment when attention of *any* kind is directed his way. He's wearing slacks, a long sleeved shirt, and hush puppies. He stares around him with a bemused expression and says "Excuse me" and "I'm sorry" and "Golly". He drives a small pickup truck with a camper shell. The tires have *whitewalls*.

We will call him gentleman "A".

Now picture a different man. Shoulder length hair, leather jacket, jeans, t-shirt, sunglasses dark enough to stop neutrons, and a pronounced tendency to stare through you like you're not there. He plays the drums in a ragged rock and roll band and the last song of every show he kicks over the entire drum set.

He has an attitude and drives a low slung motorcycle. He sweats a lot.

We will call him man "B". He is *no* gentleman.

Both of these creatures are Bradley Denton.

So what happened?

Was it moving to Texas?

No, those of you who've read *Wrack'n'Roll* know that man "B" was there in Brad back when he lived in Lawrence, Kansas (even if he did look like something from *Revenge of the Nerds*). Anyone who has followed Brad's short fiction over the past eight years knows that this savage creature has always been there, inside a calmer, more genteel facade. If you're acquainted with his latest book, *Buddy Holly Is Alive and Well on Ganymede*, you know that Brad Denton burns with the fierce fire of all true believers. And if you have the good fortune to read his James Blackburn stories, you'll know that this fire is white hot.

It is no coincidence that this book is called *A Conflagration Artist*. Yes, that *is* the name of one of the stories within, seeing print here for the first time, but it also describes Bradley as well, for reasons that will become clear as you read this collection. There is fire in most of these stories, figurative and literal, cleansing and scarring, and I assure you that you can't read these stories without feeling the heat.

And don't worry. Brad isn't (yet) a danger to society. You *can* meet him without harm, for while Man "B" is definitely in Bradley, he hasn't escaped Gentleman "A" yet. He still blushes with wonderful regularity. He still stammers from embarrassment. And he still has whitewalls on his truck.

— Steven Gould

In the Fullness of Time

Darrell (1)

The slowness begins as the pickup truck's headlight beams jump onto a boxcar. His right foot tries to stab the brake pedal, but his muscles are too sluggish. It's as if the air has turned to gelatin.

He's been driving too fast. The brakes lock too late.

But he had to get Kaye home on time, didn't he?

Alien sound envelops him as the truck fishtails. The tires groan like dying animals, and Kaye's gasp is like air filling a huge bellows.

Kaye. He forces his head to turn toward her and sees that her face, illuminated by the pale green glow from the dashboard, is twisting into an expression of fear.

He tries to say that it's all right, that he loves her, but he can't open his mouth far enough.

Another boxcar is in their path now. It's the one they'll hit. On Kaye's side.

Darrell is aware of everything, of the train, of Kaye's breath, of the weirdness of the light. The brake pedal thrums against his foot. The pickup's springs compress. There is a stink of black rubber and asphalt.

He sees, hears, feels, and smells it all. And he can do nothing about it.

They shouldn't have gone to a party so far out in the country,

so far away from the house where Mrs. Phillips watches the passage of every minute on the living room clock. He shouldn't have had the last three beers. He shouldn't have let time get away.

Not after what Kaye's gone through for him. You're only seventeen, the others are always telling her. He's twenty-two. And what kind of support could he give you driving a soft-drink truck? What about your college plans?

He looks at her frightened eyes and tries again to say he loves her. But the sound of grinding, tearing metal fills the world.

The side of the boxcar looms beside Kaye's head. Darrell sees rough speckles of paint just before the window explodes.

Green-glittering cubes shoot through the cab in a slow spray. Darrell sees Kaye try to turn, sees her mouth open, sees the particles bury themselves in her cheeks and eyes.

The roof comes down.

Nine-tenths of a second have passed since the headlights shone onto the train.

Frank (1)

He calls Lori to say he'll be home late. It's a heavy Friday night in the E/R, much heavier than usual for a town of 11,000 like El Dorado, much heavier than usual for the whole county, and he thinks he should help.

He works on a cardiac case (stupid — the guy took up jogging tonight at age fifty-four without getting a stress test), a kid who got his nose broken in a fight, and assorted other cut, bumped, and bruised people. *Spring must be the season for racking yourself up*, Frank thinks.

It slacks off around one, and he waves to the two EMTs and the nurse to let them know he's leaving.

But two ambulances scream up outside, and the drivers bring in new patients. Looks bad; a tremendous amount of red . . .

Frank goes to the first one, pulls off the sheet, and shudders.

11

He and one of the EMTs work on the girl, but it's useless. He can't help thinking that he might as well stay around to do the autopsy, since Jack Simmons, the alcoholic county coroner, will probably ask him to do it anyway.

He glances over and sees the second victim's face.

It's his brother.

Oh God, Black Sheep, what've you done now?

He feels a numbness in his solar plexus that he's never known before, but he banishes it by trying to save the girl.

Eventually, he has to give up.

Darrell (2)

He hears low, booming things, like voices from a record album playing at half-speed.

"... you ... awake?" one of the voices asks. "This ... is ... Frank ..."

It doesn't sound like Frank. Frank doesn't talk as if he were submerged in molasses.

Darrell opens his eyes and is surprised at how long it takes.

One of the three men standing over him in this white room is indeed Big Brother ...

... who made Mom and Dad proud before they died in the plane crash. Who married a girl his own age, from his own high school class. Who went to med school and made something of himself.

"Hello, Goody-Two-Shoes," Darrell tries to say. But instead of his voice, he hears another low, booming thing.

" ... accident ... last ... night ..." Frank says. "... fractured tibia ... lacerations ... concussion ..."

Darrell's temples throb. He doesn't think he can stand to hear warped voices much longer, but he has to find out —

What he already knows.

"Kaye," he says. In speaking that one syllable, he sounds almost normal.

Frank's colleagues turn away with incredible sluggishness and drift out the doorway that's several feet beyond the end of the hospital bed. Frank's face creases, and his eyelids half-close.

" . . . didn't . . . make it . . ." the molasses-voice says.

Darrell listens to blood forcing its way through the vessels in his head. It's a sound like the ocean, or a gargantuan washing machine.

"I want to see her," he tries to make his tongue and lips say.

" . . . burial . . . tonight . . ." Frank says. "Mrs. Phillips . . . didn't want . . . embalming . . . Kansas law . . . twenty-four hours . . ."

The slowness of the words is horrible.

Darrell begins to close his eyes. If only no one will talk to him, he'll be all right. The hospital stench is sickening, but at least it isn't time-warped like everything else.

He doesn't get his eyes completely closed before he sees a crying woman float into the room.

It is Kaye's mother, clutching a Bible in her left hand. She raises her right arm and points at Darrell.

"MUR . . . DER . . . ER . . ."

The word hangs like smoke.

"BURN . . . IN . . . HELL . . ."

She goes on and on, and Darrell can only understand part of what she says. But it's enough:

Kaye was only six weeks away from graduating, and then she'd have gone to college. She would have been safe. But now — now —

If her father were alive, he'd get his gun and —

Frank takes the woman's left arm. Darrell sees the fingers of her right hand curl and is surprised that Frank can't dodge quickly enough to avoid the nails that strike his cheek.

The other men return and grasp the woman's shoulders. Her wail resonates in Darrell's jaw.

The three doctors take Mrs. Phillips out of the room.

13

They walk as ghosts through water.

Frank (2)

He checks his brother's pulse, blood pressure, and respiration, then frowns and writes in the green spiral notepad he bought at the drugstore this morning.

In the past four days, he's gone through all the literature that could possibly be relevant, done blood tests, reflex tests, and even a CAT scan. All indicate that Darrell's obvious injuries are his only physical wounds.

Whatever else is wrong, then, is beyond Frank's power to heal.

At least there'll be no legal trouble. The crossing was unlit and its markers knocked down by vandals, and Darrell was only doing four miles per hour over the speed limit. The blood tests for THC and other illegal drugs were negative, and the alcohol level was below that of legal intoxication.

(Frank wonders about this, though he tries not to. The tests were done so long after the wreck . . .)

Still, just because the law won't prosecute doesn't mean that his patient hasn't put *himself* on trial.

He pats Darrell's arm and goes out to the nurses' station.

There he makes a phone call to a friend in Wichita, a friend who owes him favors. A psychiatrist.

He feels like a failure. A traitor.

Like Goody-Two-Shoes.

Darrell (3)

Raindrops drift down like elongated glass beads in clear syrup. He almost smiles as he watches them disintegrate against the sidewalk.

Then he raises his eyes. The old place looks too perfect.

Frank and Lori have painted it blue and planted shrubs and flowers to mask the concrete-block foundation. Darrell wonders if they've even landscaped the family cemetery on the back twenty.

Frank holds his crutches and helps him out of the car. *A slow ballet for cripples*, Darrell thinks.

"Good . . . country . . . air," Frank says.

Darrell wishes Frank wouldn't talk to him without using the three-speed tape recorder. It's too hard to make sense out of the grotesquely stretched words.

But then, he knows Frank only bought the recorder to humor him. Big Brother thinks the problem is mental. He's even hired a shrink, a med school buddy named Andrew Barnes.

The shrink says Darrell is punishing himself.

"Accidents . . . happen . . ." Barnes said at the hospital, refusing to use the recorder. "Yet you . . . take blame . . . delude . . . yourself . . . You . . . move . . . speak . . . essentially . . . normally . . . must . . . forgive . . . yourself . . ."

"Accidents happen." Right. A sweet, beautiful one-hundred-and-three-pound woman has been crushed by a ton of metal.

"Forgive yourself." But even if he does, Kaye's friends and family never will. Frank didn't let him attend the memorial service a week after the burial, saying it was "too soon" to get out of bed, but Darrell knows the real reason. He couldn't go because he would have been the Murderer. Murderers don't go to their victims' funerals.

"In . . . the . . . fullness . . . of . . . time," Barnes has said, "they . . . will . . . forgive . . ."

How long will that take? Darrell wonders. And how long will it *seem* to take?

He counts off seconds as he hobbles up the sidewalk behind Frank, reaching two hundred and fifty before they stand on the front porch. The sidewalk is fifteen yards long.

The year in the hospital, Frank has told him, took two weeks.

The two months he's to spend here will probably seem like a decade, because the slowness is getting worse.

It takes three hours, in Darrell's time, for him and his things to be moved into the little room on the first floor. This was his bedroom when he was a teenager, after Frank left for college, and his narrow bed, chipped maple bureau, and oak nightstand are still here. But the paisley wallpaper has been replaced by neat wallboard painted a light blue. There's also a new rag rug, speckled with bright colors. He wonders if Lori made it herself.

Frank leaves him alone "for a few seconds," so he counts the rug's colors and memorizes the position of every speckle.

Has his body slowed down, or has his mind sped up? Or have both slowed down, but at different rates?

As he sits motionless on the edge of the bed, it occurs to him that he feels normal for the first time since the accident. He's alone with no moving object to serve as a frame of reference, so his thoughts seem to progress at their proper rate. But he must remain still . . .

Only the dead can be still forever.

He begins to wonder how much time is really passing and sees that there's no clock in here. Probably an intentional omission on Frank's part.

After what seems like an hour, Frank's ten-year-old son Paul enters the room. Skinny and freckled, the boy reminds Darrell too much of what he himself was like as a kid. The resemblance is especially striking now that Darrell has time to note every blemish and scrape. The big scab on Paul's left forearm duplicates an injury Darrell had at the same age as the result of a nasty bike wreck.

He studies Paul's face and sees the hero-worship he's always seen there, now mingled with worry and fear. What must it be like to worship someone and then have your God despised by almost everyone else?

Paul touches the plaster encasing his uncle's right shin and calf. Darrell winces even though he feels nothing.

16

"No . . . basketball?" Paul asks in a voice as deep and slow as a whale's.

"'Fraid not," Darrell tries to say. His jaw aches, and he tells himself he must be imagining it. There can be no pain, for Frank and the psychiatrist insist that he speaks "essentially normally." It's only in his guilty mind that his voice has slowed.

Ah, but dear brother and dear shrink, what does "essentially" mean in doctorese?

Frank returns and tells Paul to change clothes. At least that's what Darrell thinks he says. The boy leaves.

Frank has the bulky three-speed tape recorder with him. He sets it on the floor, moves the speed switch from the first position to the second, and pushes the PLAY button. The reels seem to stare at Darrell like crazy brown eyes.

"I don't like using this," the machine says, "but I will now since Lori wants to go into town for Chinese food. We usually eat out on Saturday evening." The voice is still too slow to be Frank's, but at least it's understandable. "I know they fed you before I came up, so do you want to come, or will you be all right by yourself?"

Even in the stretched syllables, Darrell can hear what Frank hopes the answer will be. Lori was one of Kaye's teachers, and she must not want Darrell to come along, must not even want him in the house. Frank is trying to be Perfect Husband and Big Brother at the same time.

Goody-Two-Shoes, Darrell thinks as he watches Frank's finger come down on the STOP button.

"I'll be fine," he forces out. It takes ten minutes.

Frank nods in a gradual sinking of chin toward chest, then holds out a small brown bottle. The word LORAZEPAM stands out in typed capitals on the prescription label. This stuff was the shrink's idea.

"Frank says . . . you aren't . . . sleeping . . ." Barnes said when he wrote the prescription. ". . . too much . . . anxiety . . ."

But Darrell hasn't been taking it. Frank doles out the pills

17

and, trusting soul that he is, never checks to see if his brother is actually swallowing them.

Frank shakes out a pentagon-shaped tablet and puts it on the nightstand. Then he replaces the bottle in his pocket and takes a stethoscope and sphygmomanometer from the bureau's top drawer.

To Darrell's mind, the brief check on his vital signs takes about an hour and a half. When it's over, he tries to say, "Really slowing, aren't I?"

The muscles in Frank's neck ripple as he shakes his head. Then he pushes the PLAY button again.

"You say the same thing every time," the machine says, "so here's my all-purpose answer: Even if your pulse and respiration were slower than they used to be, and I'm not saying they are, it'd be the result of biofeedback. Like Andy says, once you stop punishing yourself, everything'll be back . . . to . . . normal."

The last few words are so low and drawn-out that Darrell has to guess at what they are from the context of the words that have come before. He wishes Frank would use the high-speed setting.

As his brother leaves the room, Darrell sighs. The sound is like the rumble of a freight train.

He thinks of how Kaye looked just before she died.

The little white pentagon on the nightstand gleams at him. He knows why Frank keeps the bottle, but it doesn't matter. In the pocket of a pair of jeans in his suitcase is a plastic cylinder he took from a trash can at the hospital. When he adds this latest pill, he'll have ten altogether.

Frank's wife, Lori, glides past the open doorway with the baby, Jennifer, in her arms. Her posture suggests that she's hurrying, and she doesn't look in at him. But Darrell can read the message etched in her profile. She wants him gone. She hates him, as does everyone who knows he killed Kaye. Except Frank and Paul, who are trapped by blood.

Barnes doesn't hate him either, but that doesn't count. A

shrink is trained not to hate paying patients no matter what they've done. Darrell wonders how much he'd have to pay the rest of the world to make them feel the same way.

He doesn't blame Lori. But he can't go back to his third-floor walk-up or to driving the Pepsi truck until his leg heals, can he? And until the slowness stops . . .

Paul returns with an armload of books almost as big as he is, and after a subjective hour Darrell understands that these are books Frank thinks might help pass the time. Darrell tries to say "thank you" and doesn't know if the words come out right or not. The boy gives him a long hug and then dashes out, running on the moon. Darrell's throat feels tight.

Much later, Frank appears in the doorway and indicates that he and his family are leaving. Is Darrell sure he'll be all right?

Darrell manages a nod.

Long after Frank, Lori, and the kids have gone, the tearless heaving hits him. But it isn't as bad as it was during the sleepless, week-long nights in the hospital. It only lasts a few hours.

When it's over, Darrell concentrates on his movements and is able to pick up the crutches and rise from the bed. Eventually, he makes it into the hall and turns toward the living room.

By the time he reaches the edge of Lori's new dove-gray carpet, he feels winded and sore. His breath is a rasp.

If he squints, the reddish lamplight shows him the hands of the clock that's part of the waterfall painting on the far wall. It's seven P.M. He's been back in his boyhood home for twenty minutes.

Strangely, returning to his room doesn't seem to take as long as the trip out did. Maybe, he thinks as he sinks down to the bed, Frank and the shrink are right. He'll never be rid of the pain, but if he can learn to live with it —

The stack of books is beside the bed, and the jacket of the one on top catches his eye. It looks like a slam-bang thriller similar to the ones he read in this room as a kid. He picks it up, trying to ignore the slowness of his muscles, and opens it to the first chapter.

He's gotten through less than half a sentence when he realizes the true extent of the change. He can read single words or even pairs of words with no difficulty, but when he tries to move his eyes to the next pair —

It's so painfully slow that the concentration required to move his eyes obliterates his comprehension of what he's just read. He spends what feels like four hours reading thirty words he can't remember. His head aches.

He can't watch television; he tried in the hospital, and all he saw were snowy flickers. He can't talk, can't listen, can't read — can't do anything but sit and think. And when he does that, he thinks of the wreck, of Kaye's death.

He drops the book, then rises and again makes the trek to the living room. It takes twice as long to reach the edge of the carpet as it did the first time. The aluminum crutches groan.

He stares across the room at the waterfall painting, tells himself he can't be sure of what he sees in the dim light, and ventures out farther. The crutches leave deep round wells behind him. It's like crossing a desert of gray sand, and it takes forever.

When his face is only a few inches from the face of the clock, he holds his breath until he can hear the steady hum of the mechanism.

Then he begins breathing again, and the sound is deeper and slower than ever.

It's two minutes past seven.

Frank (3)

There's only one Chinese restaurant in El Dorado, and there are no empty tables when they arrive. They have to wait in a recessed area to the right of the entrance, imprisoned behind velvet ropes.

Frank feels as though he's standing under a lens that's focusing the sun to a burning point.

"They're talking about us," Lori mutters. "Mary Webb and her husband. Terry Tucker and somebody I don't know."

Paul looks up with a puzzled expression. "What, Mom?"

Frank shifts the baby's weight from his right arm to his left. "She wasn't talking to you, kiddo." He tries to sound jocular and fails.

The waiter finally comes for them, and as Frank walks between the tables he feels as though he's running a gauntlet. Sure, Darrell used to be a little wild — drank too much beer, drag raced down Central — but do they think he killed the Phillips girl on purpose?

" . . . heard the boy driving was stoned . . ." a woman whispers to her companion as Frank passes their table.

That's a lie! he wants to shout, and holds it in throughout the entire meal.

If only they could see Darrell, or the green notepad, maybe they wouldn't —

He breaks open a fortune cookie. Of course they would. Prejudice is stronger than pity.

His fortune says, YOU WILL PROSPER WHILE OTHERS FAIL.

He waits for Lori to finish so they can leave.

Once they're in the parking lot, he feels better despite Lori's anger. At least they can go home now and spend a few hours away from other people.

As he takes the car keys from his pocket, he sees a young redheaded male leaning against their station wagon.

"Oh no," Lori whispers.

"Who is it?" Frank asks in a low voice, slowing his pace. His keys jut up between his knuckles.

"His name's Tad Johnson. He was in my comp class last quarter. He . . . sat beside Kaye Phillips. I heard him ask her out several times. She always said no . . ."

21

The teenager stands up and gestures at Frank. "You Doctor Butler?" he says loudly. "Darrell Butler's brother?"

"That's me. Excuse me; I have to get to my car." Frank shoulders past Tad Johnson and inserts the key in the lock. Lori takes the kids around to the other side.

"I got a question," the teenager says.

Something churns in Frank's abdomen. He gets in the car and reaches across to unlock the passenger door.

Johnson leans over and glares through the closed window. "Did you let Kaye Phillips die so you could save your piece of shit brother?"

Numbness crawls up Frank's chest into his neck and brain.

Is that what they think?

The rearview mirror reflects his son scrambling across the back seat.

"You shut up!" the child screams.

The teenager's face presses against the glass. "Rumor says you gave him the dope he was on. But the cops took your word he was straight, didn't they?"

Frank feels as if his head were encased in a block of ice. He starts the car's engine, guns it, and slams the transmission into gear.

Five miles down the road, he can still see an anonymous face pressed against the glass, accusing him, scorning him.

Because of Darrell. Because of his wild, hated brother.

He decides not to show the green notepad to another physician. He'll take care of his own blood.

Darrell (4)

The only trees in the back twenty are inside the cemetery fence. He touches the bark of the big cottonwood and remembers the platform he built in it when he was thirteen. It didn't last long; his mother made him take down the boards, saying it wasn't respectful to build a tree house where the dead were resting.

Darrell stands with Andrew Barnes before the single grave where his parents are buried. It's the only one of the thirty-five on the quarter acre that's still built up in a slight mound. The others are all flat, recognizable as graves only because of the headstones. Tiny blue spiderwort blossoms are everywhere. Kaye liked wildflowers . . .

A week ago — actually this morning — Barnes took him to the cemetery where she's buried. He wishes he'd had some of the spiderwort, because the groundskeeper had long since removed the other mourners' flowers, leaving a bare dirt mound that didn't even have a headstone yet. The only marker was a metal plate with removable letters, and her name was spelled wrong.

He decides to take a few wildflowers back to the house. Uprooted spiderwort tends to die quickly, but to him it'll seem to last a long time. He begins to stoop down, and it takes so long that he almost changes his mind. But at last he comes up with fifteen or twenty blossoms and looks at them closely, trying to distinguish the purplish grains of color on the petals from what must be a white background.

An hour or two later, he becomes aware of Barnes pulling on his arm.

He turns toward the psychiatrist and is struck by how out of place the other man looks. Barnes is short and nearly bald with thick eyeglasses and a black mustache, and he's wearing a dark blue suit with a red tie. The shrink clashes with the meadow, the trees, the headstones, and especially the wildflowers.

For the first time in years, Darrell feels the urge to laugh. But when he gives in to it he's immediately sorry; the sound is like a whooping foghorn.

Barnes takes the spiderwort and hands Darrell his crutches, and they begin the journey to the mile road where the psychiatrist's incongruous Lincoln sits like a monument.

As far as Darrell knows, shrinks don't usually make house calls, and they certainly don't spend Mondays driving their patients all over the countryside. Yet Barnes has been coming out to the old place twice a week for four weeks. He's being paid, but Darrell is sure he wouldn't be doing all this if it weren't for his friendship with Frank.

Just what is it about Big Brother that makes everybody want to do him favors? What was Frank born with that Darrell wasn't?

Frank is home when they reach the house, and he has Barnes stay for dinner. Darrell is glad of that, because meals are usually the worst parts of his days. His sense of taste seems unaffected by the slowness, but he has no appetite, and sitting at the table means being within the sphere of Lori's hatred. The psychiatrist's neutrality might make the hours of chewing and forced smiling more tolerable.

It doesn't happen the way Darrell envisions. Paul isn't at the table, and Lori stays only long enough to deposit the baby in her high chair and whisper something to Frank. Darrell guesses that he's meant to hear, but to him the whispering is only a series of long hisses.

Paul must be in trouble, he thinks, and for a few hours he tries to find confirmation in Frank's face. But Frank has a way of hiding concern that's especially effective now that his facial movements are so slow.

Darrell lets his fried chicken fall to his plate.

Big Brother and the shrink look at him strangely.

"Paauull," Darrell says. The vowel sound seems to fill the air for a full minute.

Low noises come from Frank's mouth.

Darrell pushes himself up from the table, grasps his crutches, and leaves. It'll take a while to find out what's wrong, but he has nothing but time.

When he reaches his room, he lies on the bed and reaches underneath to switch the tape recorder to slow-speed and start it running on RECORD.

Frank and Barnes come in a few hours later, the shrink

24

carrying Jennifer. Darrell closes his eyes and thinks of their voices as wind in distant trees. He's aware of Frank examining him, but he keeps his eyes closed.

Much later, after they've gone, he rewinds the tape and moves the speed switch to the third position. The voices are still too slow, but mostly understandable.

"I wonder if he even heard what we said." That was Barnes. "His delusion may have progressed to the point where he literally can't understand us. Perhaps —"

"No. He's not going to the State Hospital. They can't do anything for him that we can't."

Rustling sounds; Frank getting out the stethoscope and sphygmomanometer. A rip of velcro. The baby whimpering.

"How's he doing? There, there, Jenny."

"Um . . . fine."

"You don't sound like you mean it, and you keep touching something in your pocket. What is it — a memo pad? Anything I should see?"

"No . . . Listen, talk to him, will you? I don't like the way he's just lying there. Trying to mimic coma, I guess. Feel like my brother's a cadaver."

"I'll try — here, take your daughter, she's slobbering — but if he doesn't want to hear me, he won't. Darrell. A few days' expulsion isn't a punishment a boy Paul's age pays much attention to. Yes, he got into a fight, and yes, it was over you. But no real damage was done. If anything, this should serve as proof of your worth. Paul thinks the world of you. You don't want to close yourself off from him, do you?"

A long silence, broken only by a meaningless yelp from Jennifer.

Then Frank's voice again: "Andy, I can't help but wonder . . . You think there's any chance the problem really could have a physiological basis?"

"No. Not unless you blew every test, which I find hard to believe. Look, most problems of the psyche have physical components. But which is the cause and which the effect? To the patient, there isn't always a difference. To us, there must be. Otherwise we have no hope of curing."

"Yes, but —" Frank's voice stops abruptly and then starts over. "It's just that I keep remembering a car wreck I had in college. Went off a curve and down a flight of concrete steps. And it *did* seem as though time slowed down, just as Darrell describes it. I seemed to fall a hundred yards between each step."

"A trick of the mind," the shrink's voice says. "Sort of a temporary paralysis due to shock or fear, lasting only as long as the event. But Darrell connects that paralysis with what happened to the girl. He feels he must punish himself by remaining in the state he was in at the instant of her death. He'll stop when he realizes the pointlessness of that. Are you listening, Darrell?"

Another long silence.

"I don't think he needs a tranquilizer tonight, do you?" Frank's voice asks. "Like I said, he's doing a good imitation of a coma."

"He's resting well enough, but not necessarily too well, as you imply. He's just tired — limping around on crutches all day will do that, you know."

The tape recorder replays the sounds of Frank and Tony's footsteps and of the door closing.

Darrell turns off the machine and lies still. With his eyes closed, he can see what must have happened to Paul.

"Hey, how's it feel to have an uncle who kills people?"

Paul would smolder, and the next time, or the time after that —

"Looka this kid. Got killer blood. His dad does abortions, and his uncle murdered a girl. Heard she was pregnant, too. His unk's a *pregnant girl* murderer."

Paul would explode, flailing at the bigger kid's face, kicking, crying —

"He is not! He is NOT!"

Darrell's eyes sting.

Something touches his left forearm. He'd flinch, but his muscles are too slow.

When his eyes open, he sees his nephew's face through blurred air. The skin around the boy's right eye is purple, and the bruise extends down past the cheekbone. Paul's nose is so swollen that his freckles are invisible. His lower lip is split.

Darrell tries to say he's sorry.

Paul finds the tape recorder, switches it to slow-speed RECORD, and begins speaking into the microphone. Darrell watches him, wishing he could take the wounds upon his own face.

Paul is still talking when Lori appears in the doorway. Darrell feels hot beams stab into his brain.

After what must be a brief argument, Paul leaves. He pauses at the doorway, turns back, and raises a hand. Then Lori grasps his arm and pulls him out. The door shuts, and a hollow rumble makes the bed vibrate.

Darrell listens to the tape.

"Don't be mad at me like Mom and Dad, Uncle Darrell. I know I look bad, but you should see the other guy. He has a big fat lying mouth, and I closed it for him."

A long pause.

"You get well soon, and then we'll show them. I guess I'm gonna stay home tomorrow."

"Paul! You're to stay in your room until I tell you to come out, young man."

"I said I'm sorry. I feel bad for —"

"How do you think I'll feel when the other teachers ask me why my own son got into a fight at the grade school?"

"Tell them Jody Billings is a fat liar!"

"Get out here! Get away from that — that —"

In his mind, Darrell hears the word Lori couldn't say. He's heard it over and over since Kaye's mother said it at the hospital.

The sounds of small, angry footsteps come from the tape recorder.

"Uncle Darrell, I —"

"Come on!"

At this speed the rumble is more obviously the sound of the door being closed. Not slammed — Lori wouldn't allow herself that — but closed hard enough that the message is clear.

Darrell turns off the machine and thinks of the plastic prescription bottle on the floor between the wall and a leg of the nightstand. There are thirty-nine pills in it now. He wonders if that would be enough.

"Your unk couldn't stop killin', could he? But he got a busted leg when he murdered the girl, so he couldn't kill anyone else. Had to get himself. Least he won't kill any more pregnant girls, huh?"

No. Even if the other kids left Paul alone, it would be wrong. Because if the boy ever had bad trouble, really bad trouble, and offed himself . . .

That death would be Darrell's fault too.

He tries to think of other options and realizes that he has only one. To move away from El Dorado, maybe clear the hell out of the state. Then in a few years, after Paul has forgotten about him, he can do what he wants.

If only his leg would heal so he could get going. It's taking so goddamn long for the bone to knit . . . or does it just seem like it?

He broods for weeks and decides that he can't face the dry sobs, the convulsions, tonight. Just this once, he wants something he hasn't had much of for a long time: sleep. And he won't get it without one of the white pentagons.

It takes several minutes to retrieve the cylinder, but then getting a tablet is easy because he always leaves the cap loose. One pill teeters on the rim for a few moments before drifting down into his palm.

After swallowing it, he lies back and remembers the first

time he and Kaye made love, out at the reservoir one night last July. They drove around for hours before finally stopping in a wooded area of the state park. Then they spread sleeping bags and blankets in the truck bed and slowly undressed each other in the dark heat.

Slowness was good then, was wonderful, delicious. If only its permanence had begun then instead of ten months later. Those ten months would have seemed a lifetime. A perfect lifetime.

He dreams of how it would have been.

Frank (4)

When his friend has gone, he writes down the latest findings. Then he looks at all the numbers he has so far and wonders if he should show the notepad to Barnes after all. And if it would make any difference. He doesn't think what's happening can be stopped.

Something inside Darrell is changing him beyond what even grief and guilt should be able to do, and the part of Frank that is a doctor wants to tell his colleagues about it whether they can help or not. But the part of him that is Darrell's brother . . .

He puts off the decision by going into his study to sort through the day's mail. Lori has already taken out the bills and junk mail, and what's left is a pile consisting of three brochures from pharmaceutical companies, a request for money from his alumni association, and a postcard from a vacationing friend.

There is also a second pile: Four envelopes addressed to Darrell. A little better, Frank thinks; the day before yesterday there were six.

He opens the first. Inside is a single sheet of paper covered with huge block letters:

DIE YOU DRUG BASTURD SHE WAS WORTH 10000000000 OF YOU I HOPE YOU DROUN IN YOU'RE OWN PUS. IF I CATSH YOU OUTSIDE I WILL KILL YOU.

The other three are longer, and worse. The worst of all is the last one Frank opens. It is neatly typed, grammatically perfect, and contains no obscenities. It suggests that Darrell castrate himself with a piece of broken glass.

Frank tears them up. But more will come tomorrow. Tonight is the night Kaye Phillips would have graduated from high school.

The people of El Dorado wouldn't be satisfied if Darrell really did go into a coma. They want nothing less than his death.

After a few minutes of hesitation, Frank opens the telephone directory and copies several numbers into the green notepad. It's time to buy the things he'll need.

He isn't sure how he knows that. But he knows.

Darrell (5)

He raises himself up on one elbow, feeling as groggy as if he'd slept for several weeks. And to his mind, he has.

Frank is here, and he puts the tape recorder on the bed beside Darrell's left hand.

"It's good to see you sleep," the thick machine-voice says, "but I'm going to have to wake you. Lori can't get a substitute because the seniors graduated last night, and some of them trashed her room. It's finals time for her juniors, so . . . you get the idea. And I've got five hospital patients I've got to see, plus appointments, so I can't stay home either. Jenny's day-care center won't take Paul, and we couldn't find anyone to sit with him. He's going to have to stay home.

"He's under strict orders not to leave the house or turn on the stove. But just in case anything should happen, dial number seven on the hall phone. That's preset to my paging service, and they'll beep me. Okay?"

Darrell looks up at Frank. "O . . . ," he begins, and decides it isn't worth the effort.

Frank shuts off the tape recorder and checks Darrell's pulse.

He frowns and seems about to reach for the tape recorder again, then leaves. Darrell watches him as he goes. Frank's wearing a dark brown three-piece suit and looks every inch the successful doctor.

Goody-Two-Shoes, Darrell thinks, and sits up. He's slept in his clothes and feels grubby. And slow. Frank seems to have been gone for six hours before Darrell's feet touch the floor.

Three sounds like the beats of distant tympani quiver in the air. Someone is knocking on the half-open door.

He's surprised to see that it's Lori. Frank caught a good-looking one, Darrell thinks as she glides toward him. Shoulder-length honey-blonde hair, hazel eyes . . . but she can't compare to the dark, quiet beauty that was Kaye. Nobody can.

Lori picks up the microphone, rewinds the tape, and begins recording. Darrell has nothing to do for a long time but watch her, and he doesn't have to understand her words to know what she's saying.

He feels as though he's baking.

Days later, she goes out without looking at him.

"I have nothing against you . . ." the message begins.

She despises him.

" . . . but you're reckless. Please don't take this the wrong way. I hate leaving Paul here today, but I don't see any way around it. I'll be home as soon as I can. What I'm trying to say is that if anything happens . . . I'm holding you responsible."

Only fair, Darrell thinks.

"And I know your leg's a problem, but . . . could you please go back to your apartment? It'd be better for everybody. You too; you need your independence."

Even as slowly as the words come out of the speaker, Darrell can tell that the last sentence was spoken as if Lori had been saying "You need to stab yourself."

He rewinds and erases the tape. Tonight he'll tell Frank that he wants to move back to his own place tomorrow. The hell with the stairs. The twenty-four hours remaining in his stay should only seem like a month or so.

A day later, after the journey back from the bathroom, Darrell sits on the bed and stares at the powder-blue wall, thinking of how Kaye's hair curled below her ears.

Then Paul comes in. He's carrying a cassette recorder, but he uses the three-speed to tape a message.

The boy's face looks worse than it did yesterday. The lids of his left eye have swollen into purple half-moons.

When Paul finishes talking, he rewinds the tape and changes the speed selector switch. Then he presses the PLAY button and sits silently while Darrell listens.

"Mom told me not to bother you, but you won't tell, will you? I was in my room fooling around with my record player, and I got an idea. I don't know if it worked. If it didn't, you can throw away the tape. It's kinda neat being home without Mom and Dad, even if I do have to stay inside. We were s'posed to have an arithmetic test today, but Mrs. Clinton said she'd let me make it up if I didn't blab about it. I don't think she likes Jody either . . . So I guess I better go now since Mom said I shouldn't come in here unless I was dying. This is your nephew Paul signing off. Roger wilco, over and out."

When the message ends, Darrell strains his facial muscles into a grin. Paul grins back, looking a little pathetic, then turns on the cassette player and bounces out of the room.

Darrell is surprised to hear recognizable music. It's still too slow, but the song is clearly an old Willie Nelson number. Paul has played a thirty-three-and-a-third RPM album at forty-five or seventy-eight and taped the result.

Darrell looks down at the Magic-Markered letters on his cast: PAUL THE GREAT WAS HERE XXX. Next to the words is a drawing of a stick figure with a cape.

After listening to both sides of the tape, Darrell starts it again at the beginning. He wonders how he can begin to repay his nephew for the gift.

Then he realizes that the song he's listening to seems slower than it did the first time through. Some of the words are slurred. Maybe the batteries . . .

He finds an AC cord in a compartment on the back of the cassette player and plugs it into the socket beside the nightstand.

The music still sounds slower than ever.

Before the first side has played through for the second time, Darrell can't recognize the songs. He raises his head and is frightened at how long it takes.

His eyes focus on the jar on top of the bureau. The spiderwort he picked yesterday is dead.

Frank (5)

He has made his phone calls and written two checks, but the notepad in his jacket pocket still seems to generate enough heat to burn through to his heart. He knows he's not paying enough attention to his patients today, knows he's not being a good doctor. He hates it.

He wishes he knew what to do beyond what he's done, wishes there were some way to test what he thinks is happening, wishes he could know whether his own silence indicates strength or cowardice. But he doesn't believe wishes come true.

He doesn't belive in premonitions either. Yet he has acted on one.

At lunchtime he checks his box outside the hospital's mail-room. Inside is an envelope addressed to SCUM'S BROTHER.

He throws it away without opening it.

Today, he thinks.

Let it be today.

Darrell (6)

He lies on the bed with his right hand on his chest. He can't feel a heartbeat. When he tries to lift his right arm, it feels as though it were wet clay.

Just as his hand begins to rise, he becomes aware of a moaning sound, like the vibrations of thick power lines in a storm, and has the unshakable feeling that it's calling him.

The sound grows louder as he fights to make his muscles take him out of bed. He tries to count seconds as he begins to move toward the door, but he loses count after three hundred. His arms and legs feel numb, and he can hardly control the crutches.

By the time he reaches the gray desert, he knows the sound is coming from the porch. The front door is open a few inches.

The moan throbs as if it were his missing heartbeat. It's the only thing he's aware of, the only thing he feels. The crutches swing past his body as if part of a huge, slow, cosmic gear.

When he's finally crossed the desert, he leans on his left crutch and uses the right one as a pry bar.

The door pivots as if it were a slab of stone. When it's open halfway, Darrell sees Paul on the porch, his mouth open wide, his bruised face contorted in rage and pain. The moan isn't a moan at all, but a scream.

A seventeen- or eighteen-year-old stranger is behind Paul, holding the child's elbows. Three other teenage males are turning toward the door. Darrell recognizes two of them. One is a beefy, redheaded guy named Johnson who Kaye said was always bothering her. The other is one of Kaye's cousins.

Darrell begins pushing the screen door open with his crutch, and he smells soured beer.

He knows what's happened. The seniors graduated last night. Kaye was probably eulogized, and these guys have been cursing the son of a bitch who killed her. Somewhere toward morning they decided that if the law wouldn't get him, they would. He deserves to have his shit kicked to hell, one of them would say. She dies and all he gets is a busted leg and a cushy place to flop. He's alone there during the day . . .

The moaning gets louder and higher in pitch before it's

overpowered by the sound that comes from Johnson's mouth:

"MMMUUURRR . . . DDDEEERRR . . . EEERRR . . ."

Kaye's cousin reaches for the screen door.

Darrell sees it all coming, coming even more slowly than it did the night of the accident. And like that night, he can do nothing to stop it.

Johnson drags Darrell out onto the porch.

Paul is struggling. He must have heard them and come out to see who it was. If only he'd stayed inside. If only he hadn't gotten into the fight at school. If only Kaye hadn't died . . .

The crutches drift down and bounce off the narrow boards. It's as if they've fallen to the surface of a tiny wooden planet.

A fist comes toward Darrell's face. The fingers are tanned and thick, the knuckles creased like dry leather. A silvery thing with a red stone hits him below his left eye.

He feels nothing at first. For a few minutes it's as if his face simply tries to change shape.

Only when the blow is long past does the pain come. It starts as a fuzziness at the edge of vision, then creeps in until all is dark except a white-hot point at the center.

Then that point bursts, and its fragments shred tissue as if they were pieces from the window of Darrell's pickup truck.

The boards of the porch press against his right shoulder until his collarbone aches. A cold metal tube burns across his cheek. As the momentum of his fall turns him onto his back, he tastes a thick, metallic saltiness. It's as if he's been chewing green copper.

The blackness flows back to the periphery, and Darrell sees Paul kick the ankle of the stranger holding him.

The teenager stumbles back, still clutching Paul, and falls off the edge of the porch. An hour later, he lands on the boy, pinning him against the sidewalk.

Darrell begins yelling, and the sound is exactly like Paul's scream. He tries to get up, but Johnson's foot kicks him back down.

Before a second kick can land, Darrell finds a crutch and

rams it into Johnson's groin. Then he swings it at the other two, and they jump off the porch to float down like cottonwood seeds. The one who fell on Paul is getting up, and Darrell sees that the child's lower right leg is unnaturally bent.

Johnson stumbles off the porch after the others, and they run away as though they were crawling.

Darrell tries to go down the steps on one crutch and falls, landing beside Paul. The boy's face is wet with tears and blood.

Gradually, Darrell pushes himself up to his knees, leaving the crutch on the ground, then slides his right arm under Paul's thin shoulders and his left arm under the boy's thighs. The lift takes hours.

When Darrell has Paul cradled against his chest, he brings up his left knee until the ball of his foot is against the sidewalk. Then he tries to drag his weighted right leg upright.

They fall twice. The moan is constant. But Darrell finally stands.

Pain stabs up his right leg as his plaster-encased foot presses down on the first porch step. It feels as if he's breaking the bone all over again, one cell at a time. The boy in his arms has the weight of a mountain.

It takes a day to climb the three steps to the porch.

Ten hours to reach the screen door.

Three days to open the door without dropping Paul.

A week to cross the gray desert.

Another week to lower the boy to the couch.

A year to find the hall telephone.

He feels nothing, hears nothing as he searches. He tastes blood. He misses Kaye.

He is in a slow universe, alone.

Frank (6)

He hangs up the phone and, hating himself, hopes this will be it. He hopes Darrell would understand, and that Paul isn't badly hurt.

He doesn't know if he believes in hope or not.

He calls Lori, then rides to the house in the ambulance.

Darrell (7)

It's dark outside his window.

Frank is talking to the shrink, who is standing in the corner looking unhappy. Lori is in the hall outside the doorway, her face in shadow. That's good, because Darrell doesn't want to see it.

Paul is in his room upstairs, asleep. Darrell imagines him lying there, his face discolored, frowning at a bad dream and trying to turn onto his side. But he can't because of the cast on his lower right leg.

The tape recorder is in PLAY mode on its fastest speed, but Darrell can't make out any words. Barnes has given in to the "delusion" only to have his surrender be meaningless.

It doesn't matter; Darrell knows the litany: "These things aren't your fault. It would be foolish to feel guilt over the acts of others . . ."

He thinks he also knows the subtext:

"I don't understand this. You're breathing too slowly. Your eyes move only at long intervals, and your hands move hardly at all. Yet there's nothing physically wrong with you. We'd know if there were, we would, we would . . ."

Sure, shrink. Nothing's wrong. Nothing's ever been wrong. A little kid got hell beat out of him and a shattered leg because of me. Big deal. I killed the woman I loved. Double big deal.

Sure, shrink. Everything's great. You don't stand like a wooden statue. Frank doesn't take a month to scratch his arm. Let's all run to the back twenty and dance on the headstones.

Even as Darrell thinks, he knows his thoughts are slowing down to match his body. Two real-time days ago, he relived four years of high school while Frank took his blood pressure. Now, Barnes's long message has concluded before Darrell's

37

finished imagining what it might be saying.

He has perceived the world as moving in slow motion, and his brain is finally adjusting to follow suit.

He wonders how it is that his *perception* has been operating at a rate different from his *thoughts* in the first place. Isn't perception simply the interaction of thoughts and senses?

He doesn't know, and he's too tired to try to figure it out. If he were able to hold a conversation, he'd put the paradox up to Barnes. But if he were able to hold a conversation, there wouldn't be a paradox . . .

Frank and the shrink have left the room and closed the door. It took them about six weeks.

The forty-six days since Kaye's death have been twenty years. Twenty years to relive the moment when the glass bits tore into her cheek. Twenty years to beat the face of a child and snap the bones of his leg.

Darrell's thoughts are interrupted by the aroma of roast beef. He focuses on it, savoring something undistorted.

Yet he can't imagine eating the meat. His slow body has no need of energy.

He tries to listen to his heartbeat and hears nothing. He tries to listen to the blood pushing through his head and still hears nothing.

Eventually thought itself is too difficult. All that's left is smell, and even that fails him when the aroma of the roast beef fades away.

He longs to dream as he did last night. In his dreams everything's normal — he can race someone, fight someone, make love to Kaye. Even nightmares are better than the thickness of his waking hours.

With a tremendous effort, he makes his eyelids close. And then he waits. In silence. In nothing.

But again sleep won't come on its own. Unless he can swallow a white pentagon, he'll lie awake, unable to move or even to think, for years.

Move, left arm. Down off the bed.

Nothing happens until he's repeated the command a hundred times. Then, numbly, his left arm slides toward the edge of the mattress.

Two more inches. Come on. Two more inches.

At last his arm falls over the curve of the sheet. A few minutes later, his knuckles scrape across the floor and bump against a leg of the nightstand.

Back. Back a foot. Over and over again.

By the time his fingers close around the cylinder, his whole body is sweating.

Up now. Up. Up. Please, please, up.

Eventually the message trickles down slow nerves to his arm muscles, and the pill bottle begins to rise.

How many should he take this time? he wonders. He wants to sleep long enough to dream of loving Kaye and playing basketball with Paul, deep enough to forget what he's done to them.

A shudder rumbles through him as his hand rises over his face, and blackness reappears like a ring surrounding his vision.

Is this sleep? Do I need —

The cylinder tips, and the loose cap tumbles off like something ejected from a spacecraft.

Mouth open, concentrate —

The pills drift out and fall around Darrell a thousand times more slowly than snowflakes in still air.

The blackness washes over him, and he feels inexplicably, wonderfully peaceful.

Frank (7)

He stands with Barnes outside the door to Darrell's room. The psychiatrist is biting his lower lip and staring at the floor. Frank, not knowing if he should, has given in and shown his friend the contents of the green notepad. He's glad that Lori is already upstairs in bed.

He opens the door and sees white flakes on his brother's chest.

He has the stethoscope out of the bureau drawer and is beside Darrell in an instant, searching for a pulse. He's aware of Barnes standing anxiously behind him.

"Nothing," he mutters as if it were a curse. He's about to start CPR and tell Barnes to call for an ambulance, then stops himself.

"Give me your watch," he says instead.

"I thought you couldn't find a pulse," Barnes murmurs.

"Give it to me."

Barnes hands him the watch, and Frank holds it close to Darrell's lips.

"What in —" Barnes begins.

"Shut up and count the pills," Frank says.

The psychiatrist obeys. "Thirty-eight," he announces after half a minute.

Frank does some swift arithmetic, then says, "Go to the bathroom and flush them down the toilet."

He looks up and sees his friend staring at him. "I'll do no such thing," Barnes says.

"See if you hear anything, then." He moves aside but keeps the watch half an inch from his brother's slack mouth.

Barnes takes the stethoscope and tries for three minutes.

"He's gone, Frank. No heartbeat, no respiration."

"Right. Drug overdose."

Barnes scowls. "If these are the tabs I prescribed, he hasn't taken any. One, maybe."

"He took them all. Flush them down the toilet."

The psychiatrist pulls off the stethoscope and looks away. "The county coroner will want an autopsy."

Frank shakes his head. "Four times, I've done post-mortems for Jack when he was too drunk to do them himself. I'll fill out and sign the death certificate, and he won't question it."

"Do you know what you're doing?"

"You saw my notes."

"And I can't believe your conclusions."

"Believe this," Frank says, and holds up the watch.

The crystal is fogged.

Late the next afternoon, Frank buries Darrell next to their parents. He has a brief moment of doubt as he uses the rented backhoe to scoop a thin layer of earth over the fiberglass canopy that was once a boat, but it goes away quickly. There is no life in the land of Hate. Happiness for the despised must wait until Hate is forgotten.

Seven times, he drives the backhoe into the pasture and scatter-dumps the leftover dirt. Then he walks back into the cemetery and looks beneath a clump of spiderwort behind his parents' headstone to be sure the battery is connected properly. The ends of two hoses are hidden beneath the same clump, and he holds his hand over them for a half-second.

When he stands up, he sees that he's finished just in time. Barnes is bringing Lori and the kids in from the road.

They aren't religious, but Frank reads the twenty-third Psalm anyway. Its words have an eerie significance, and he finishes in a quavering voice.

Paul hobbles over to the big cottonwood and leans against it, crying. Frank can't think of what to say; he knows the boy can't understand yet . . .

Darrell should've been Paul's father, he thinks.

Lori is beside Frank, holding the sleeping baby, and he feels her looking at him.

"I saw the time written on the receipt," she says, half-whispering. "You paid the deposit on the backhoe yesterday morning. Early."

"I was thinking of putting in a new septic tank."

Lori's eyes don't flinch. "Yourself? Who'd take your patients?"

Barnes makes uncertain noises in his throat.

"You got the casket awfully quickly," Lori continues, "and

you cut through the paperwork as if you knew just what to do so you could bury him yourself and avoid embalm —"

"I've buried family before."

She seems about to argue, then looks over at Paul, who has dropped his crutches and pressed his forehead against the tree trunk. Her expression changes.

"He needs you now," she says.

Hesitantly, Frank goes to his son and puts his hands on the boy's shoulders.

"Just remember him," he says hoarsely, "and he'll never be gone."

Paul turns and hides his bruised face against his father's chest.

Andrew Barnes picks a handful of spiderwort and puts it on the bare mound of earth.

"From the shrink," he murmurs.

After several minutes of silence, they begin walking back toward the road. Frank lags behind to close the gate.

The spiderwort bundle on Darrell's grave is being scattered by a gust of wind.

"When I learn what it is," Frank says too quietly to be heard, "and when those who hate you are gone . . ."

He leaves the sentence unfinished.

Rest well, Black Sheep. I'll be back tomorrow evening. And the next evening. And the next. And if it takes that long, Paul and his children . . .

He latches the gate.

Rest.

And in the shade of the cottonwood, Darrell rests, dreaming slow dreams of love throughout the century that will pass before his next heartbeat.

Top of the Charts

The transubstantiation of *Homo sapiens* was nowhere in my thoughts the first time Doctor Joe came into the shop. He was wearing a three-piece suit with a little flag pin in the necktie, and my immediate reaction was that he didn't belong in Electroshock Records and Tapes.

The Pretenders were blasting out "Bad Boys Get Spanked" from all four corners, and Doctor Joe's face twisted in pain. But his eyes radiated determination as he walked up to me at the counter and said something.

"What?" I asked.

He said something again. Reluctantly, I reached behind me and turned down the volume.

"Thank you," he said stiffly. "I am Doctor Joseph Wright, and I would like to see the manager, young lady."

"You're looking at her, elderly sir," I said. He wasn't old, maybe mid-forties, but ever since I was three it's ticked me off to be called "young lady," even by somebody too stupid to realize it's insulting. "The store owner is in the Bahamas and has left me in charge. May I help you find anything?"

Doctor Joe looked displeased. "If you're in charge," he said, "does that mean you're in charge of *everything*?"

I reached behind me and turned up the volume a little. Doctor Joe winced.

"Yeah," I said. "I've been running the place for seven months. The owner doesn't like customer interaction."

Doctor Joe opened a briefcase and removed two white

posters with black lettering. "I'd like you to put these in your front window."

I held out my hand for them. We put up posters for almost anything — chili feeds, concerts, Druid prayer vigils, whatever. There was always room for a few more, if I took down those that were six months out of date.

Usually I didn't give them half a glance, but the block letters of Doctor Joe's posters jumped out at me:

WARNING TO PARENTS AND THEIR CHILDREN: MANY OF THE RECORD ALBUMS IN THIS STORE CONTAIN SATANIC MESSAGES CONCEALED BY THE SUBLIMINAL TECHNIQUE OF BACKWARD MASKING. BUYING AND LISTENING TO THESE RECORD ALBUMS IS DANGEROUS TO YOUR MENTAL AND SPIRITUAL WELL-BEING.

Doctor Joe was already heading for the door. I lifted the stylus off the Pretenders, and the silence stunned several browsing patrons.

"Halt, Fascist," I said to Doctor Joe's retreating backside.

He spun around. His face was red, and with a fleshy face like his, that was a lot of color.

"Just kidding," I said as he returned. "Just trying to get your attention."

He put both hands on the counter and glared at me.

I regretted calling him back. I'm five-three and weigh one hundred and seven. Doctor Joe was at least six-two and weighed — well, imagine a water buffalo in a three-piece suit.

"You see, sir," I said as my fingers fumbled with the chain of the whistle I always wear, "I cannot place these posters in the window. Even were their statements true, your imagined complaint would be with the record companies. We're only a retailer."

He took them back. "May I demonstrate something?"

I thought about it.

"No," I said after a tenth of a second.

He came around the counter.

"No customers are allowed on this side of the register," I said, backing away from him. "I have orders to call the authorities."

He went to the turntable. I'd turned it off, but the amplifier was still on.

Doctor Joe placed the stylus in the middle of a track and spun the Pretenders backwards.

The windows nearly broke.

I hadn't been kidding when I'd said that my boss didn't like customer interaction. He liked it so little that he had long ago put a sawed-off softball bat under the counter. I chased Doctor Joe out of the store with it.

"Give me a chance to prove my claim!" he shouted once he was across the street.

"Give me a chance to crush your chitin!" I yelled, and went back inside to call the police.

The officer I talked to emphasized that he wouldn't be surprised if there *were* Satanic messages on the records I sold.

"I sell Satie and Stravinsky too, you know," I said.

"Twisted punks," the officer replied. He then told me that Doctor (of Divinity) Joseph Wright was pastor of the largest television congregation in the region and a highly respected man.

"He's a Looney Tune," I informed the officer, who hung up on me.

I sold a couple of cutouts, a Bach cassette, and a copy of the new Mangled Orphans EP, and pretty soon I began to feel better. If Doctor Joe was really respectable, he wouldn't come back. Kansas City boasted at least thirty classier record stores that he could terrorize to his heart's content.

At eight o'clock my night clerk, BooBoo (who wouldn't respond to his real name even when I remembered it), came in to take over. I told him about Doctor Joe.

"Wild," BooBoo said. "Wild" was BooBoo's response to

everything from pancakes to the threat of nuclear vaporization. Some would have considered him to be a little on the defective side, but he knew the lyrics to everything Bruce Springsteen ever wrote.

I showed BooBoo where the sawed-off softball bat was in case Doctor Joe tried to make a nighttime raid.

BooBoo seemed to like the bat. "Wild," he said.

I left the store in his capable hands and drove to Randall's apartment. Randall was the least degenerate of my boyfriends, and after a day of Electroshock patrons, a nice, quiet, neo-classical cheese-ball-eater was just what I needed.

We sipped white wine and listened to Rachmaninoff. I told Randall about Doctor Joe, and he was sympathetic. He didn't care for progressive music, but he knew that rock didn't resort to tricks like backward masking.

"It perverts the masses quite well enough without that," he said.

I hit him with a sofa pillow.

"You're an extraordinarily exciting woman, Terri," he said.

"You're an excruciatingly boring man."

"Yes, and you love it, too."

After a while we got back to the subject of Doctor Joe, and I worried about what I'd do if he came back.

"Let him put up the posters," Randall suggested. "After all, how many of your patrons can read? And even if the 'warning' is noticed, will that deter anyone? People love to buy things that are bad for them. Witness the megabucks pulled in by tobacco, alcohol, pot, cocaine, and diet soda."

I realized he was right and called BooBoo at the store.

"Listen," I said, "if Doctor Joe comes in, don't give him any trouble. Put up the posters. Use our tape."

"Wild," BooBoo said.

"I mean it," I said, afraid that BooBoo didn't understand. "Be nice. Be his buddy."

"Tramps like us," BooBoo said. "Baby, we were born to run."

I hung up, and Randall and I continued our pleasant neo-classical evening. Sometime after two I drove home to my own apartment, playing the Stones on the car tape deck. I wondered what "Sympathy for the Devil" would sound like backwards and decided it didn't matter. Human civilization was wonderful.

Doctor Joe came back the next day while I was putting out new albums. This time he carried a portable record player.

"Doctor Wright," I said, smiling my best I'd-love-to-lick-your-shoes smile, "of course we'd be glad to put up your posters. We of Electroshock Records and Tapes believe in public service."

Doctor Joe frowned and went to the counter. I followed, afraid that he might break something. I had a stack of albums in my hands, and if worst came to worst, I could use them to deck him.

He put the record player on the counter, removed the lid, and opened his briefcase. "I know you only want to get rid of me, young lady," he said.

I felt my upper lip curling back.

"However," Doctor Joe continued, "this time I'm not leaving until I perform a demonstration. I'm as concerned for your soul as I am for the souls of your customers."

I thanked him profusely and asked him to go right home and pray for me for a week or two.

He paid no attention and found a socket to plug in his record player. "This turntable is belt-driven," he said, "and I've put a twist in the belt so it runs backwards." He took a copy of *Buddy Holly Lives* from his briefcase and cued up "Not Fade Away" at the end of the track.

"Now listen," Doctor Joe said. "You can quite clearly hear the words, 'Come kiss Satan on the lips, perverse children of the Eighties.' "

He played it and gesticulated vigorously when the phrase occurred. I had to admit that if I tried, I could hear words. But they were something like "Use two cups of flour and ice-skate naked."

I suggested that since Buddy Holly had been dead for a quarter of a century, he could have no desire to make the children of the Eighties kiss anybody anywhere. Doctor Joe huffily noted that Satanic powers weren't bound by the grave.

I was more convinced than ever that Doctor Joe would be most at home in a chapel with flexible walls.

"Thanks for everything," I said, helpfully unplugging his record player. "I'll put up the posters if you'll leave them."

He looked at me disapprovingly. "You don't seem to appreciate the seriousness of this," he said. "This is brainwashing direct from Satan by way of his Communist puppets in the popular music industry."

I wished BooBoo were there to quote Springsteen; that would get rid of the Revered Gentleman if anything would.

Doctor Joe stared at the albums I'd put on the counter in order to free my hands for shoving him toward the door. His face grew purplish, and he pointed.

"You see?" he said. "You see now? They're even admitting it."

The first album in the stack was a debut release by a new band called The Interstellar Peace Project. Lousy name for a group, I thought. The cover was bad, too — a lot of stars and galactic gunk shaped like a dove on a black background.

What had Doctor Joe upset was a white sticker in the lower right corner that I hadn't noticed before. It said "gniksaM drawkcaB gninraW."

"Well, I'll be damned," I said.

"I know, I know," Doctor Joe said excitedly. He picked up the album and turned it over to read the back. In a few seconds he shrieked.

I looked at the title his quivering finger was trying to point at: "The Pan-Humanistic Backward Bop."

"Humanism!" he shouted. "Communism!"

49

"Fluoridation!" I added.

I charged him $9.98 for the album, two dollars more than our usual discount price. He left ecstatic because he'd really be able to work his viewers into a frenzy with *this*.

I was glad to be rid of him until I saw that he'd left his record player.

Resigned to yet another evangelical visit, I went back to putting out new albums. As I worked, I realized that I was filing an awful lot of Interstellar Peace Project records. It wasn't smart to stock that many copies of a debut album until the band proved itself.

I took a copy to the back room to check my files, and I noticed that it didn't have the white sticker.

By the time I finished going over my carbons, it had dawned on me that I had fifty copies of an album I hadn't ordered. And according to my invoices, the distributor hadn't shipped it.

I made some phone calls, and after an hour of the usual Distributor's Wrangle, I got the following explanation:

I did not have any Interstellar Peace Project albums.

Au contraire, I informed the drug-abusing lackey on the other end of the line. I had fifty of the things.

I was told that was not possible for two reasons:

One, the albums had never been shipped.

Two, they did not exist.

Did that mean I could keep them?

I could pulverize and inhale them for all the lackey cared. I thanked him and blew my whistle before hanging up.

The album cover didn't list band personnel, a copyright date, or a label imprint, and the labels on the disk itself only named the five songs: "Learning to Love Crustaceans," "The Pan-Humanistic Backward Bop," "Your Stalk-Eyed Friend," "Bureaucratic Mind Candy," and "My Way." I hadn't heard any of them on the radio yet. Usually the jocks got things a few weeks before I did — but then, they didn't necessarily play them.

I put the record on the shop turntable, hoping for something commensurate with the album's mysterious appearance, and was disappointed. It wasn't bad; it just didn't blow my brain out through my ears the way I'd imagined it might.

The vocals were heavily filtered so the songs sounded like they were being sung underwater by androgynous elves — odd, but not much different from a lot of top forty stuff — and the merely competent instrumentals relied heavily on synthesized hums and rumbles. The lyrics were arcane, but, again, not really weird for rock:

Your baby is a beauty
She lives inside a shell
She's one of several million
Interstellar Personnel
You've got to learn to love her
All you backward human nations
Learn to give it up to love her
Learn to love real big crustaceans

I figured that if the band got any airplay, I'd be able to sell twenty of the fifty copies — maybe a few more if I cut the price. I'd gotten them for nothing, so any sale at all was profit.

I left the record playing and began to file more albums. Almost immediately, I had a sensation that felt like three dozen cockroaches running down my spine. I shuddered and looked around, expecting to see Doctor Joe.

Instead, I saw that all my patrons were standing still with their mouths hanging open. That wouldn't have bothered me if the phenomenon had been confined to two or three of them, but there were fourteen customers in the store, and every one of them was as animated as a popsicle. After a few seconds I realized that each was staring at the corner speaker nearest him or her.

Okay, it was new stuff they hadn't heard before. No big deal. I approached the patron nearest me and shouted in his ear.

"Like it?" I said. "Just got it in today."

His irises seemed to flicker, but he didn't look at me. When he spoke, his voice was a subdued monotone that was difficult to sort out from the music.

"So beautiful," he said. "So beautiful to be at peace with my friend and her beautiful green shell with eyes like pearls and tail like the terraces of heaven."

"I beg your pardon?" I said.

The track ended, and he looked at me.

"I want that album. I'll pay whatever you say."

"$7.98," I said.

By the time I got to the register to ring it up, all fourteen zombies had crowded around to buy the Interstellar Peace Project album. Their staring eyes made me nervous.

The next track began to play. It was the one Doctor Joe had shrieked about, a real rocker:

Well, make your pappy happy
Don't make your mama cry
You gotta all be ready
When the ships come from the sky
You gotta back it on up
Shoo-wop, shoo-wop
You gotta back it on up
Shoo-wop, shoo-wop
Turn your bullets into gravel
Slow your run down to a walk
'Cause everybody's gonna do
The Humanistic Bop

Each zombie became a dancing maniac, like Howdy Doody on speed. They were still able to get money out of their pockets, though, and I no longer felt like the potential main course in a George Romero film.

But I didn't feel exactly comfortable.

BooBoo came in at eight. His eyes looked a little glazed, but I tried not to worry. His eyes always looked a little glazed.

"BooBoo," I said tentatively as I sold another IPP album. "Have you ever heard of a band called The Interstellar Peace Project?"

BooBoo nodded somberly and killed the stereo system. Then he reached up and switched on the television, which was permanently tuned to the cable rock music channel.

BooBoo turned toward me and jerked his thumb at the screen. "Wild," he said.

"I can't get enough of this," the VJ was saying in a drunken stupor, "and I know you can't either. So, for the forty-ninth time today, but who's counting, here's The Interstellar Peace Project and their new release, 'The Pan-Humanistic Backward Bop.' I wanna have these guys' babies, how about you?"

The video was of the surreal variety, and the dominant images as the music played were of flowers, dancing sheep, and indistinct giant lobsters.

I watched for a while and then shrugged. It was pretty typical stuff.

"I've sold thirty-two of those albums today," I said, "and I don't even know where they came from. I don't get it." I peered at BooBoo's eyes. "Do you?" I couldn't tell if he'd been turned into a zombie or not.

BooBoo shook his head. "Nice, but it ain't Springsteen."

I was taken aback. I hadn't heard BooBoo vocalize anything besides "Wild" and Springsteen lyrics since he'd said "Thanks for the job."

"That's a relief," I said. "I was afraid that everybody except me was being brainwashed just like Doctor Joe said."

BooBoo snapped off the television, and the store was quiet. For the first time all day, there were no customers.

"Much as I hate to say it," BooBoo said, concentrating hard on forming the words, "he may be right in this case. I have a

Master's in psychology, and —"

"You didn't mention that on your job application."

One corner of his mouth curved up. "I thought it'd keep you from hiring me. Anyway, I've watched that video twenty times since noon, and I can't help but see it as a subtle attempt at behavior modification."

I was staring at him. "You can even say big words."

He nodded. "One way to condition a subject is by anchoring a desired situation or behavior with positive, behavior-reinforcing actions or images. In that video, what I'd consider positive images occur during lines of the song that seem to be trying to convince the listener to accept something."

I didn't ask what, but he told me anyway.

"The strongest anchoring," he said quietly, "if that's what it is, occurs when the band is singing about ships coming from the sky."

We were both quiet for a few minutes. I tried to convince myself that BooBoo had always been off his nut and was only now displaying the complete symptomatology.

But I'd never heard of IPP before that morning, and neither had he. Neither had anyone else. Even the Beatles had cranked it out in dives for a few years before hitting the top of the charts.

The Interstellar Peace Project had done it in a day.

Well, what if they had? With the right packaging, the advertising industry could have made Queen Victoria a teen idol. Or even Doctor Joe.

"Look," I said, "we shouldn't get paranoid. After all, Americans blow millions on sugar water every year because of a few sexy commercials. Whoever these guys are, they've just got a great manager who's getting them incredible PR and distribution, that's all. It's not impossible, not with enough money."

"Wild," BooBoo said. It was a reassuring sound.

I didn't want to waste any more time worrying about a pop craze; I had a date with a cheese-ball-eater. I took care of a few things in the office, gave BooBoo a pat on the back, and headed for the door.

Randall came in before I got there.

I knew him well enough to know that he would never willingly come to Electroshock Records and Tapes after dark. Something was wrong.

"I'm not due at your place for ten minutes," I said, checking my watch. "What're you doing here?"

Randall grasped my shoulders and gazed into my eyes.

"Peace and love, sister," he said. "We await the crustaceans."

I looked back at BooBoo.

"Now," I said, "we should get paranoid."

I tried to stop him, to talk to him, to find out what had happened to him and to God only knew how many others, but he wouldn't stay. I considered using the bat, but I could no sooner have clobbered a delirious hamster.

He'd been buying groceries that afternoon and had heard the Bop while selecting cheese. Now he was going to a rally at the football stadium and wanted me to come along. The fans of The Interstellar Peace Project were going to play the album over the public-address system and memorize the lyrics.

I felt the sick realization that I'd never have a nice, quiet evening with him again.

He left without me. I stood looking after him through the dirty plate glass until he was obscured by a chili feed poster.

Too wiped out to go home, I walked back to the office. I could feel BooBoo watching.

I closed the door behind me, lay down on the black Naugahyde couch, and tried not to think.

After finally dozing off, I dreamed of giant lobsters singing of peace and love. I was chasing them with a forklift truck and trying to drop them into a swimming pool filled with boiling water. But just as I got one into the steam, it turned into Doctor Joe. I dropped it anyway.

Then I had my usual dream in which my mother asks me why I'm not married yet. But toward the end her head turned into a cheese ball.

My eyes shot open, and at first I didn't remember where I was. The light that came into the office through the cracks around the door was weak and bluish. I got up and stumbled out into the shop.

The overhead lights were off; the blue glow came from the amplifier. BooBoo was sitting behind the counter with his head in his hands, listening to a song about cars and girls. The volume was low, and the place seemed more peaceful than it ever had before.

"BooBoo?" I said softly. I didn't think he'd seen me yet. "What time is it?"

He answered without moving. "After one."

"Why're you still here? Closing time was over an hour ago."

He shrugged his shoulders.

"Many customers tonight?" I asked.

He picked up an album from the counter and waved it. I couldn't see what it was, but I didn't have to. "Last one," he said.

I went behind the counter and sat beside him on the other stool.

"What's going on?" I muttered. "When somebody like Randall switches from Rachmaninoff to underwater elves, something unnatural is happening."

BooBoo shrugged again. In the faint blue light, I could see that he was lip-syncing along with Springsteen. He probably wasn't even listening to me.

He'd put the last IPP album back on the counter. It was too dark to see the illustration clearly, but I ran my fingers across the plastic, thinking that maybe I could feel what made this so different from everything else.

My fingers stopped at the lower right corner.

There was nothing there. But in my mind's eye, I'd been

56

running my fingers over the first IPP album I'd noticed, the one I'd sold to Doctor Joe.

"Gniksam," I mumbled. "Drawkcab. Gninraw."

"Wild," BooBoo murmured.

I spun around to lift the tone arm off BooBoo's album and accidentally sent the stylus skittering across the tracks.

BooBoo buried his face in his arms.

I found Doctor Joe's record player under the counter next to the softball bat, ripped open the IPP album, and put the disc on the backward-playing turntable.

"Sorry about your record," I said as I plugged in the player, "but this is important."

BooBoo raised his head and looked at me. I could just make out the faint glistening in his eyes that said nothing was more important than Springsteen.

I had to ignore it. If I was right, BooBoo would understand soon enough.

I cued up the stylus at the end of "The Pan-Humanistic Backward Bop" and flipped the switch to the ON position.

The sounds that skreeked out of the cheap little speaker were horrible at first, and they stayed that way. I was about to turn it off to save our ears when voices pierced through the cacophony.

"Greetings to you," the voices said. It was another chorus of underwater elves. But they weren't singing.

"We estimate that no more than four percent of your population will be able to distinguish these words," the voices continued. "You are those who are not affected by the subsonic stimuli encoded into our songs and who will therefore examine this music to determine what has happened to the other ninety-six percent. If you are intelligent enough to find this message, you are intelligent enough to deserve an explanation. And to listen to reason.

"You may not have noticed, but you people are making a terrible mess of things. Sorry to be blunt, but we don't believe in thrashing outside the shrub.

"Indeed, your race is so maladjusted that you are a threat not only to yourselves but to other intelligent species in the Galaxy.

"Because of ethical considerations you wouldn't understand, we can't blip you out of existence. Because you're not at all nice, we can't leave you alone. Curiously, there are a few dissenters in the Galactic Community who feel that we should continue allowing you to develop on your own — but, happily for all, we have overruled them. It's clear that you can only get worse if left to yourselves.

"Thus we have to correct your flaws without turning you into non-sentient plantlike organisms.

"To that end, we're infiltrating each of your cultural divisions with what most will think is music. All over the planet, subsonics are implanting peaceful impulses and erasing nasty ones. Only the packaging varies.

"The apparant blank stupidity of those affected is temporary. It's easiest to shut down most intellectual functions during modification.

"Unfortunately, we can't seem to develop a sequence of subsonics that will affect all of you. So we must settle for a majority and try to reason with the rest. With you.

"We believe you'll be valuable members of the Galactic Community once your defects are eliminated. We expect that to be accomplished within three of your years. Give or take a couple. There are many variables.

"One variable is you who hear these words. Two years after the Project's initiation, we'll send ambassadors to assess your reactions. You'll find that we're pretty nice, despite the fact that we evolved from sea creatures similar to some you frequently boil and devour.

"You have a history of wishing for peace, and now you're getting it. If you have questions, we've phrased all this in slightly different terms on the other tracks.

"Have a moderately enjoyable day."

I turned off the record player and looked at BooBoo. Even

in the dark, I could see his lips pursing to articulate a "W."

"Please don't," I said, and he stopped himself.

It was so silent then that all I could hear was the blood pumping past my ears.

We both believed it. I believed because it would take an alien power to make Randall change. BooBoo believed because it was easier than not believing.

"So what do we do?" I said finally.

BooBoo started his Springsteen album again.

He meant there was nothing to do but what we'd always done. We hadn't been able to transform the world ourselves, so now it was time to let someone else take a shot at it.

"Peace will be good," I said.

It sounded stupid. What did I know about peace or war or anything in between? I'd been brought up in a safe Midwestern middle-class home; I'd majored in Music Theory in college for three years; I'd worked in Electroshock Records and Tapes for three more years. The closest I'd been to the horrors of human strife was the evening news.

I knew that we screwed up a lot, but I hadn't experienced any of it firsthand.

So I began to feel more afraid of what the aliens said they were giving us than I was of our nasty impulses.

I must have been saying all of that out loud, because BooBoo put his hand on my arm and stopped me in mid-thought.

"I've seen some of it," he said. "They're right. We're despicable." He didn't elaborate.

"Can we trust them to make us any better?"

BooBoo didn't answer.

In any case, what could I do about it?

I went back to my Naugahyde couch.

I felt lousy in the morning, and I avoided smooth surfaces so I wouldn't risk seeing my reflection. BooBoo didn't look good either. The smart thing to do would have been to stay closed, but I didn't feel like doing anything smart. I was grubby and grouchy and foul-breathed. I was nasty, and I wanted to share it with the Galaxy.

BooBoo stayed around. I asked why he didn't go home, but he only smiled. He looked as if he was expecting something to happen and didn't want to miss it.

Sure enough, Doctor Joe came back.

"Greetings, brother and sister," Doctor Joe said. "We await—"

"Yeah, yeah," I snarled. "You await the coming of the crayfish." I shoved the portable record player across the counter at him. "Take it. Although you probably don't care about Satanic messages anymore."

Doctor Joe smiled pleasantly. He could actually look like a sweet guy. It scared the hell out of me.

"I have seen the error of my ways," Doctor Joe said softly. "It is far better to focus on good than to search for evil."

"Uh-huh," I said. "Take your machine and blow."

His face took on an expression of deep concern. "Sister Terri, what's wrong? Don't you feel well?"

I was about to comment upon his mother's disappointment when something in my chest squirmed.

"How did you know my name?"

Doctor Joe smiled benignly and spread his hands in a gesture of gee-I-don't-know-I-guess-we're-all-brothers-and-sisters.

On impulse, I plugged in his record player, put on the IPP album, and played the same passage that BooBoo and I had listened to the night before.

"Do you hear it?" I asked Doctor Joe.

"Hear what?" he said, his voice dripping molasses.

I reached across the counter and got him by the necktie. "The backward message. From the aliens."

Doctor Joe shook his head. "All I hear is noise. That's a beautiful song, but only when it's played properly."

I removed the record and tried to make Doctor Joe take the player again. He looked at it as if he'd never seen it.

"If you didn't come for this," I said nastily, "just what do you want?"

He opened his briefcase and pulled out new posters: DOCTOR JOSEPH WRIGHT'S SUNDAY MORNING SHOW, "THIS HALLELUJAH HOUR OF OURS," IS CHANGING ITS FORMAT AND WILL NOW BE ENTITLED "LEARNING TO LOVE CRUSTACEANS."

I said I'd post them, and Doctor Joe walked out happily, promising to come back and buy IPP's next album when we got it. He'd heard about it on the radio.

"There's going to be *another* one?" I moaned.

"Wild," BooBoo grunted.

A customer came in about noon that same day. He was a wizened man who looked terribly angry.

"You!" he shouted, pointing at me. "You work here?"

I admitted it.

"Good," he snapped. "I can't find anything on the radio except that junk about dancing backwards. Play something else for me and I'll buy it. Beethoven. Chuck Berry. The Plasmatics. Anything."

So there were others in town who were unaffected. I put on a Chuck Berry album and played "Johnny B. Goode."

"Primitive," the man sighed as the twanging of Chuck's guitar reverberated off the walls. "But music for the universe. There's a recording of that song on Voyager I, you know." He smiled at me. "By the way, I'm Alan Michaels. I teach physics at UMKC. Or did until yesterday, anyhow."

I hadn't known about Voyager, so he told me. When the probe was being prepared for launch, a group of scientists had decided to go a step beyond the Pioneer plaque. They'd prepared a gold-plated recording of Earth sounds and music in case a spacefaring race millions of years in the future came across the thing. "Johnny B. Goode" was the only rock-and-roll song included.

So Chuck had written a song for the stars. As the idea sank in, I thought of ten or twelve other songs that, for my money, were in the same category.

We didn't need alien noise to save us, did we? Despite all our nastiness, didn't we create music that could beat anything any giant lobster ever imagined?

When Chuck was finished, I played the backward message for Professor Michaels. He was frowning when it began, and by the end of the track his eyes were shooting death rays.

BooBoo looked concerned. "Professor," he said, "you're thinking something nasty, and I want to suggest that you think again. It's not pleasant to have our destiny controlled by another species, but it may be necessary."

The Professor's expression softened slightly. "Maybe. But the struggle for survival on this world forced us to evolve into mean, tricky creatures. There's no reason to expect any other world's dominant species to evolve any differently. It may be that these, ah, crustaceans are making us docile for some nefarious purpose. All we have to convince us otherwise is their say-so. Those in positions of power have lied to us before."

BooBoo acknowledged that but still felt we should take the aliens at their word. After all, if they were trying to conquer us, they wouldn't provide a recorded explanation, would they?

The Professor suggested that the recording might only be more evidence of how tricky they were.

BooBoo responded with Springsteen lyrics he felt were appropriate. The Professor tried to provide an intelligent rebuttal, but it wasn't easy.

I stopped listening. They each had their points, and they had gotten me thinking.

Only one IPP album had displayed the white sticker. It had only been because of Doctor Joe that I'd noticed it at all. And it was only because I'd had his rigged record player that I'd tried to find the message.

How had it happened that Doctor Joe had first come into the

shop babbling about backward masking only one day before the musical invasion had begun?

It was almost as though he (or someone controlling him?) wanted to make *sure* I got the message.

It was almost as though I had been chosen.

For what purpose? And by whom?

The backward message had said something about "dissenters" in the Galactic Community . . .

I blew my whistle loud enough to make BooBoo and the Professor stop arguing.

"Either one of you may be right," I said. "So we have to prepare for either situation."

They looked at me quizzically, and I explained.

Professor Michaels is analyzing the waveforms of the IPP songs. It's a complicated study, but two years should be enough time to figure out what the "subsonics" are. We'll use his results when we enhance our weapons.

BooBoo and I are collecting the songs we'll need if we have to launch a counterassault. He's going a little overboard on the Springsteen, but I'm not complaining.

Randall came in yesterday afternoon to see if we had the second IPP album yet. We did; a case of them showed up two days ago. I don't mind selling them. After all, they might be doing a lot of good.

On the other hand, I won't sell one without taking the opportunity to test the raw, unenhanced power of our own arsenal.

I tried Rachmaninoff when Randall walked in, and it had no effect. Then I tried Dylan. Nothing. Bach. Zero.

Then, as he was leaving, I put on one that Professor Michaels suggested, another of the Voyager songs.

"Dark Was the Night," by Blind Willie Johnson, recorded in 1927. It's instrumental blues, one man and a guitar that cries and moans. Pierces right into my stomach.

Randall paused at the door and looked up at a speaker. His face lost its blank happiness for a millisecond, and I saw the music reflected in his eyes. Then he was gone.

Maybe I'll have another quiet evening with him after all. Someday.

This morning, Doctor Joe came in for the same reason as Randall. I tried Chuck Berry. Then Mozart. Then one that always makes me feel like balling up my fists and shaking them at the Powers That Be.

Angry, revolutionary stuff from The Who. "Won't Get Fooled Again."

I turned it up loud, and the store shook with rebellious feedback and Daltrey's gravelly shouting.

Doctor Joe didn't stop smiling as he looked at me and said something.

"What?" I asked.

"Are you sure you won't get fooled?" he yelled.

I turned it up until my ears hurt.

Doctor Joe went out. As I looked out the smudged window, I thought I saw him give me a thumbs-up sign.

Maybe he came back to make sure I'd heard what I was supposed to hear.

Well, whoever he is, whatever side he's on, I heard.

By the time the "ambassadors" from The Interstellar Peace Project come, we'll have found enough Unaffecteds to smuggle our enhanced records into radio stations. And to put them on the air at a moment's notice if they're needed.

We sent music to the stars. We can still hit the top of the charts.

For the time being, though, I'm giving the Project the benefit of the doubt. In two years, I'll be here to meet them with an olive branch in my hand.

And just in case, a bucket of melted butter under the counter.

Killing Weeds

Monday. Dad bangs on my bedroom door at five-thirty and calls, "Up an' at 'em, Phillie." I'm already dressed, though, and sitting on the edge of the bed to put on my oldest pair of tennies. The smell of bacon told me it was time. It's Dad's first full day back from summer camp, and we have a lot to do. Knowing him, I'll bet he's already fed and watered the calves in the lot behind the barn.

I go to my dresser to get the birthday presents he brought me — a camouflage jacket and a mother-of-pearl-handled four-blade pocketknife. I turned twelve last week while he was out in western Kansas teaching guys how to shoot howitzers. Seems like my birthday always falls during summer camp.

I complained about that to Mom, and she laughed, saying it was "an appropriate tradition."

"After all," she told me, "he was off being a soldier when you were born, too."

That started her on the story about how they got engaged just before Dad was drafted, and how after a year Grandma gave her the money to fly to Manila so she could marry him while he was on leave. "And that's how we picked your name," she always says at the end. It's her favorite story, and I've heard it at least a thousand times. Dad rolls his eyes every time she tells it when he's around.

This year he called from Fort Riley and told me that 1980 is a turning point for me. Whenever he's gone now, he says, I'm the man of the family.

Mom smiled her that's-nice-dear smile when I told her that. She thinks I'm still her baby, and won't even let me run the old John Deere 50 unless Dad's here to watch.

I heard them arguing about that last night, just two hours after he got home. I listened at the furnace vent in my bedroom floor.

"Most twelve-year-olds have been running tractors by themselves for three years already," Dad said.

"Most twelve-year-olds aren't as small as he is," Mom said.

"What does that have to do with it?" Dad asked, almost yelling. "Hell, he's damn near as good with the Allis as I am, and all I'm suggesting is that he could run the Deere with the weed-wiper or bean-bar once in a while."

"The bean-buggy, maybe, since somebody else has to be there anyway, but not the pipewick. I don't want him out in the field by himself."

"Yeah, and that's why we've got this weed problem."

"No, dear, that's because your wonderful cousin didn't take care of it two weeks ago like he said he would."

There was a long stretch of silence then, and finally Dad said, "You sound like you think that's my fault."

"I can't count how many times you've called Billy unreliable," Mom said. "We've got to face facts, Loren — if we want the farm to work, you'd better quit the Guard."

"You know damn well the only reason we haven't gone under is my Guard pay."

"Then maybe we should get jobs in town."

"Just like that, huh? They're handing them out like candy at a parade, are they?"

"We could try. We can't hold onto the farm forever, and you can't pretend everything'd be all right if only I'd let poor little Philip drive the tractors while you're out Guarding."

I was so mad at Mom that I got into bed and put the pillow over my head so I couldn't hear her anymore.

It's not my fault I'm not built big, like Dad is. Maybe I would be if Mom would get me that Olympic weight set I keep asking for.

But, hell, I don't need muscles to run a tractor. On a tractor I'm as strong as anybody.

"Get down here and eat your breakfast, you lazy kids," Dad yells from downstairs. I slip my new knife into my back pocket and put on the camouflage jacket. It'll be too hot for it in a few hours, but I want to wear it while I can.

I beat Jodi downstairs, and she screams that I pushed her. Mom is busy trying to get Crissy to stop crying, though, so she tells Jodi to shut up, sit down, and eat her eggs. Jodi whines, but Mom gives her the no-back-talk-or-else look. Jodi is eight, but she acts like as much of a baby as Crissy, who is three.

Dad is already sitting at the head of the kitchen table, chewing a mouthful of bacon and listening to the morning news and farm report on WIBW-Topeka. He winks at me when I sit down, and I dig in to catch up.

"Where's Patricia?" he asks after a minute.

I swallow a big glug of milk to wash down a lump of toast. "Still in bed, I guess. Want me to go get her?"

He shakes his head. "No, Jodi'd better do it."

Jodi whines, "Oh, Daddeee, I just sat dowwwwwn."

"You get upstairs and get your sister, or you won't be able to sit down at all, young lady."

I stuff a bunch of scrambled eggs into my mouth so I won't laugh.

Jodi stomps upstairs, clomp clomp clomp on the wooden steps, and the noise makes Crissy cry louder.

"Jodi Lee Bundy, you straighten up or you'll wish you had!" Mom yells.

Mom is in a bad mood. I think it's because of the argument. Or maybe it's just because Crissy is screeching her stupid pink head off.

Dad and I finish our breakfasts, and then we grab our Co-Op hats and walk out across the packed dirt of the barnyard to the west shop. The sun is just coming up, all orangey over the thick band of trees down in the Coal Creek valley a mile east, and the eighty-acre soybean field just this side of the creek looks like a giant, dark green carpet. There's some low, wispy fog down by the trees, but it looks like the field itself will be fairly dry. It's been five days since the last rain, and that wasn't much.

The calves in the pen behind the barn start bawling when they hear us. Dad says, "Sounds like your sisters," and makes me laugh.

He shoves open the west shop's big sliding door, and the corrugated metal rumbles like thunder. The six-row planter, the chisel-plow, the pipewick rig, and the bean-buggy — the bar folded in the middle so that the two pairs of fiberglass seats are facing each other — are lined up against one wall, and most of the rest of the shop is taken up by the John Deere and the big diesel Allis-Chalmers, its front-loader raised high.

I notice for the first time that the collapsed sunshade-umbrellas on the bean-buggy look like furled flags.

Dad stands with his hands on his hips for a few seconds, "sizing up the situation" like he always does.

"Tell you what," he says, hitching up his jeans a little. "You check the 50's oil and gas her up. By the time you've done that, I'll have the Allis out of the way so we can manhandle the bean-bar and hook 'er up."

"You got it," I say, like I imagine his troops saying when he gives them an order, and I run over to the old green John Deere. The oil is fine, so I climb up into the seat, pull the hand clutch, and hit the starter. It takes the engine a half-minute of cranking, but then it fires up, blup-blup-blup-blupblupblupblupblup. I put it in first gear, cut back the throttle, and ease out of the shop nice and slow. I hope Mom's looking out the kitchen window.

I keep the tractor in first as I drive past the barn toward the east shop. The sun is up over the trees now, and I have to squint.

I fill the 50 from the three-hundred-gallon gas tank outside the east shop, and it makes me feel good when I glance back and see that Dad isn't bothering to keep an eye on me. A few months ago, even, he would've watched to make sure I didn't use the diesel tank.

I feel the vibration in my chest when he starts the Allis and backs it into the barnyard. It's as big as an armored personnel carrier.

It takes Dad awhile to get the buggy coupled to the Deere — the hookup's more complicated than most, because the buggy has to stick out in *front* of the tractor — and then he's got to mix the herbicide and water in the buggy's seventy-five-gallon plastic tank. After that he has to tinker with the compressor and test all the wands, so by the time we're finally ready to go, it's after eight o'clock. I've been playing mumblety-peg in the barnyard with my new knife, but now I put it back into my pocket and run to the house to see if the others are ready.

Dad drives the 50 with the folded-up buggy a half-mile south down the dirt road to the bean field gate, and the rest of us follow on foot.

Patricia is complaining. She's a year younger than me, and as far as I can tell she's not good for much except teaching Jodi how to whine. "If we weren't going to have to be ready until *now*," she says, "why'd we have to get up at *five-thirty?*"

"You didn't get up at five-thirty," I tell her. "Everybody else did, but not you."

"Oh, well, you're *per-fect*, aren't you, Phil-ip?" she says, mostly through her nose.

"Both of you shut up," Mom says. She's carrying Crissy to keep the kid from crying, and she isn't happy about it.

By the time we catch up to Dad at the edge of the field, he's got the halves of the bean-bar folded out and locked in place. Now the tractor-plus-buggy rig is shaped like a T, with the bean-bar forming the crosspiece. A couple of the hoses to the wands are tangled, so I straighten them out.

"Attaboy," Dad says, talking loudly so I can hear him over the idling tractor.

Patricia gives me a dirty look.

Mom puts a cutesy little sunbonnet on Crissy, and Dad takes the kid up onto the tractor seat with him. The rest of us take the four bean-bar seats — Mom and Jodi on the left side of the tractor, Patricia and I on the right. Mom and I have the outside seats, the best ones, and we both open our sun umbrellas.

"Okay," Dad shouts, idling the Deere down a little further. "Be sure to aim low for the cockleburs. Don't get any on the bean plants if you can help it. Forget about the volunteer corn; I'll have to get it with the wiper after I take care of the milo."

"Okay, Dad!" I answer, and pop the four-foot wand out of its bracket on the side of my seat. It feels good in my hand. Broadleaf weeds, prepare to die.

"Patricia Kay and Jodi Lee, put up your sunshades!" Mom yells.

"Oh, Mo-ther!" Patricia whines. "It's chilly out here as it is."

"Put up your sunshades *now*," Mom says.

"But I want to get a tan!" Patricia whines.

"Me too!" Jodi says, like an echo.

"I'll tan both your butts if you don't do what your mother says," Dad hollers, and I can't help laughing.

"You be quiet," Mom tells me.

Brat One and Brat Two finally open their umbrellas, and Dad cranks up the Deere and takes us into the beans.

I aim the wand carefully and squeeze the trigger. A faintly purplish, fan-shaped spray shoots from the nozzle, spitting death onto the nutrient-sucking cockleburs and morning glories that are trying to take over our field.

The soybean plants are over a foot high, which means we're doing this about three weeks later than we should be. But all through the second half of June the big Angus steers kept getting out of the north pasture, and Dad and I had to fix over a quarter-mile of fence. By the time we finished that, it was time for Guard summer camp, and another two weeks were lost.

Dad's cousin Billy was supposed to weed-wipe the milo, at least, but, like Dad says, counting on Billy is like a legless man trying to count on his toes.

It ought to be all right, though. We might lose a little yield in both the beans and milo, but it's not going to be a disaster. Just like everybody else, Dad says, we do the best we can — and you can't do any more than that. In about a week, we'll have a hundred and sixty acres of prairie hay ready to mow a few miles west of here, but if this spraying isn't done by then, the hay'll have to wait.

The beans really need the help. There are so many cockleburs crowding up against the stems of the plants that I have to keep my spray going constantly. It's not hard, since I can switch hands, but the job was more fun last year. Then the weeds weren't as thick, and I had more opportunity to develop my aim. It became a game to see whether I could hit the cockleburs without getting any of the spray on the beanplants or the ground. I had to stay alert.

This year, though, there's no variety, and the grumble of the tractor and the perpetual hiss of the wands combine into a monotonous hum that makes me drowsy. As the sun rises higher and the air gets warmer, the smells of gasoline, herbicide, and bean plants swirl together and almost put me over the edge into sleep.

But then the rig jerks and stops, and even though we've been going real slow, I have to grab my chair to keep from falling off. I hear Jodi shriek, and I see that she's taken a tumble. She isn't hurt, because it's only two and a half feet to the ground, but she's plenty mad. If I'd been driving, I'd be getting an earful about now.

I look back at Dad as he cuts the tractor engine.

"What is it, Loren?" Mom asks, and she sounds so worried that I begin to feel worried myself, even though I don't know why I should.

"Quiet," Dad says, and stands up, holding Crissy against his chest. She yowls, and he puts his hand over her mouth.

"What for?" Patricia asks.

Dad takes his hand away from Crissy's mouth and points toward the north end of the field. "There," he says. "Do you see something moving down there?"

All I can see are soybeans.

"What am I supposed to be looking for?" Jodi asks, sounding really hacked-off.

"Don't speak to your father in that tone of voice," Mom says.

Dad is squinting, searching the field. "Somebody's in the beans."

"I don't see anything, dear," Mom says.

Dad shakes his head. "You don't know how to look."

"Maybe it was a coyote," I say.

Dad doesn't answer.

"Philip's probably right," Mom says. "A coyote could be staying low, or could even be in the trees by now."

Dad frowns, then sits down and restarts the tractor.

We continue spraying the rows of beans. Crissy continues bawling.

It's after ten-thirty and we're working about sixty yards from the trees when Dad kills the engine for the second time.

"Listen," he tells us, and this time we all hear it. Someone is shooting a rifle down by the creek, on our land. The sharp cracks come quickly, one every eight or nine seconds.

I feel like hitting something. We've posted signs on all the fences: NO HUNTING; NO TRESPASSING. Yet some illiterate fools, as Dad calls them, are down there anyway, looking to get us or our cattle killed.

"God damn it," Dad says, and gets down from the tractor, leaving Crissy squalling on the seat.

"Loren, I've asked you not to curse in front of the children," Mom says.

"Yeah, Dad," Patricia says, smirking. "After all, Jodi and I have Bible School this afternoon. And then we're going to see Aunt Sue, and you know what she always says about swear words."

I was through with Bible School last year, thank goodness. I don't care if I never see construction paper or hear another verse of "This Little Light of Mine" for the rest of my life.

Mom glares at Patricia, and if she weren't so far away, I think she'd smack her. "When I want a comment from you, young lady, I'll ask for it," Mom says.

Dad begins walking toward the trees.

"Loren," Mom says, "just what do you think you're doing?"

Dad slows and half-turns back toward us. "I'm going to politely tell them to get the hell out. Be right back."

I hesitate for a second, knowing that I'll get in trouble with Mom, and then I jump down from the bean-buggy and run after Dad. Mom yells for me to come-back-this-instant, but I pretend I don't hear her. She has to take the girls to Topeka in a few hours, and by the time she gets back she won't be mad anymore.

I catch up with Dad at the edge of the field. He asks, "Who invited you?" but doesn't tell me to go back, so I head into the trees with him.

It's shady and shadowy in here, a jungle of walnut and hedgeapple trees, climbing ivy, and gooseberry bushes. I remember that Mom promised to make gooseberry pies if I can ever get my sisters to help pick.

The gunfire sounds really close now. Dad yells "Heyyyy!" between each shot, to let the illiterate fools know we're looking for them, but no one answers.

We find the three of them on an old cowpath near the creek. They're standing in a patch of shade that half-hides their faces, but it looks to me like one is ancient, one is about Dad's age, and one is only a few years older than me. They're all dressed alike, in hunting vests and caps of such a dark brown that they

73

almost look black. You'd think the illiterate fools would wear something bright to keep from shooting each other. Each one carries a rifle.

Now that we've stopped moving, I realize for the first time how steamy it is down here. My camouflage jacket feels hot and itchy. Gnats are trying to fly into my ears, and when I slap them away it sounds like a bomb has gone off in my head.

"Howdy," Dad says to the strangers, being polite just like he said he'd be.

The oldest one is chewing snuff, and he spits before answering. "Howdy," he says, but he doesn't sound friendly. I don't think he has any teeth. "How're y'all doin' today?" His voice gives him away as being from Texas or somewhere else south of here.

"Just fine," Dad says, stepping a little closer to them. I hang back, not because I'm scared, but because Dad's in charge. "My family and I are spraying our beans, and we heard your guns."

"Uh-huh," the old man says, shifting his snuff. "What you sprayin' 'em with?"

Dad doesn't answer for a few seconds, but then he says, "2,4-DB."

The old man makes a snorting noise and spits again. "Why don't y'just use sugar water? Ain't gonna stop nothin' unless you use somethin' with some kick to it."

Dad seems to grow a few inches. "I use what most folks around here use for cockleburs."

"If you say so, Joe. Sorry if we made too much noise."

"Well, that's all right," Dad says, "but I'm afraid I'll have to ask you to go somewhere else."

"We're hunting whitetails," the one Dad's age says. "Cain't seem to find any, though."

Dad's super-mad now; I can tell by the way his jaw sticks out farther. "In the first place," he says, "it ain't deer season, and in the second place, you don't have permission to hunt here. You've blown off at least thirty rounds in the last minute and a

74

half, and that's too damn dangerous with people so close."

"Thought we might as well shoot some squirrels," the youngest says.

Dad takes a deep breath. "I hear any more of it, I'm calling the sheriff."

The old man swallows loudly, and grunts. "Everybody 'round here as unfriendly as you, Joe?"

Dad stiffens. "My name ain't Joe," he says, and turns to look straight at me. I can see in his eyes that he wants me to get back to the field *now*.

I turn and head back, fast.

"Nice lookin' boy," I hear the oldest hunter say. "What is he — eight, nine?"

I'm smashing through bushes now, but I can still hear Dad say, "I want your names."

"Charlie," the old man answers.

I find another cowpath and head toward the field. My run slows to a walk, but my heart still feels like a sledgehammer hitting stone. Something moves in the weeds at the edge of the path, and I remember Dad saying that there are copperheads down here. I wish I were wearing something tougher than almost-worn-out tennies.

An oval piece of tire tread, about nine inches long and four wide, is lying in the middle of the path. I pick it up with my right hand and slap the tread against my left palm. I LEFT my job, I LEFT my wife, I LEFT my friends, I LEFT for life —

I'm worried about Dad, and I think maybe I should go back to him, but I don't know what I could do if I did. I'm too God damn small. A twelve-year-old should weigh more than seventy pounds.

I step out into the field about thirty yards north of where Mom is standing with her arms crossed. Patricia, Jodi, and Crissy are still on the bean-buggy.

"Where's your father?" Mom demands as she walks toward me.

75

"Talking to the hunters," I say. My voice sounds high-pitched and thin.

"What's he saying to them?" Mom asks. "What are they doing here? What's that in your hand?"

I don't try to answer everything. I just say, "A piece of tire I found."

Mom frowns at the chunk of rubber. "How on earth did a tire get into all that brush?"

Then, as if by magic, Dad is with us. I didn't even hear him coming out of the trees.

"Let me see that," he says, and I hand him the piece of tire.

He looks at it for a long time, and the longer he looks, the madder his eyes get. I feel like something is my fault, and I have to look away from his face. My eyes focus on the tire-chunk, and I notice for the first time that there are four dirt-clogged holes near the edges of the rubber, two toward each end of the oval.

"What happened in there?" Mom asks.

Dad doesn't answer. After another couple of seconds, he turns and throws the piece of tire back into the trees.

After we've had lunch and Mom has taken the girls to town, Dad mixes glyphosate herbicide in the pipewick's two fifty-gallon tanks, then hitches the wiper to the back of the big orange Allis. He's put new ropes through the grommets in the twenty-foot horizontal plastic pipe, and he lets me use my birthday knife to trim the ends. You have to be sure that enough rope sticks out of each hole so that you get most of the Johnsongrass, but not so much rope that you're dripping a lot of poison onto the milo — sorghum, some people call it.

When Dad kicks up the idle on the Allis, thick black smoke spurts from the exhaust, making the barnyard smell "like a truck stop." Then he touches one of the hydraulic-control levers, lowering the front-loader a few feet so he can see where he's going.

"Ought to take the damn thing off," he says, "but it's too

76

much trouble. Besides, I've been thinking that I might spread some new gravel on the driveway."

Everything that needs doing around here, Dad can do. And does.

I ride on the tractor with him, sitting on the built-in toolbox (which Dad welded into place himself) beside the right fender. As we roar down the road past the soybean field, I can see waves of heat jiggling over the beans nearest the trees. I take off my camouflage jacket and tie its arms around my waist.

The road curves around Bald Hill, which blocks my view of the bean field, and then we chug down into the creek valley and across the low-water bridge. Dad slows the Allis way down and stares off down the creek as we cross the bridge. I think his mind's still on the hunters.

The canopy of trees over the muddy little strip of water reminds me of a tunnel. There is a stink of something dead here. A muskrat, maybe.

The trees thin out again a few dozen yards past the bridge, and the first of our two sixty-acre milo fields comes into view. It seems less orderly than the bean field, because the beans are all in neat rows, while this looks like a prairie of thick-stemmed, foot-and-a-half-high grass. Actually, the milo is planted in rows, too — it's just not so obvious from the road.

A lot of taller, scroungier-looking grass is scattered throughout the field, sticking up from six to ten inches above the crop. This stuff is Johnsongrass, and if we don't get rid of it, it'll rob the milo of nutrients just like the cockleburs are robbing the soybeans.

Dad sizes up the situation and shakes his head. "Hope we aren't too late," he says, and eases the tractor and weed-wiper across the shallow ditch into the field.

Once he opens the tank valve so that the herbicide will drip off the ropes, there isn't much to do except drive slowly up and down the field over and over again, making sure we don't miss anything or overlap the previous strip too much. Grasshoppers fly up in front of us like tiny helicopters trying to escape the enormous, crushing wheels.

After turning to start the fourth pass, Dad takes a thin cigar from his shirt pocket and lights it with a butane lighter, filling my nose with the smell of sweet tobacco. Mom won't let him smoke anywhere near her. I watch the slim brown stick burn all the way down until there's less than an inch left, and I can tell that Dad really enjoys it. He stubs it out on the left fender and tosses it into the field, then winks at me.

I know what he means: This is our little secret.

The afternoon gets to be a "real steamer" the closer we get to the creek, but we've got a three-gallon cooler of iced tea with us. If you tossed back enough iced tea, Dad says, you could march across the Sahara Desert with a full pack and come out the other side ready to put a fence around the whole thing.

I wish I could think up the kind of stuff he can.

I also wish I could be more help. All I'm doing is riding up here beside him, as if that were work. I could run the Allis and weed-wiper well enough to do the whole field myself if I had to, leaving Dad free to finish the beans — but with the women in town, we don't have enough people to ride the bean-bar. Dad considered hiring some kids for a couple of dollars an hour, but decided that we can't afford it. We'll get it done ourselves, he says, or we won't get it done at all.

We'll make it. We'll wipe every God damn weed off every God damn acre, and come fall we'll bring in the best crop we've ever had. Wait and see.

About two o'clock, Dad stops the tractor and stands up, staring off toward the trees, which are about a hundred yards away.

"You see that?" he says, and points.

I climb up to stand on the right fender. I look where he's pointing, and I see a movement in the milo.

"Think it's another coyote?" I ask, and then I see something rise above the green. It looks like a flattened cone made of straw.

I give a yell, but it's already gone. We keep watching for a few minutes, but the only motion in the milo is from a weak puff of west wind.

Dad sits down again and looks at me, his eyes serious. "What did you see?" he asks.

I tell him, and his jaw widens and sticks out the way it does when he's just about mad enough to break something. For a minute I'm afraid that I'm in trouble, but then he says, "Okay, Phillie. You keep an eye out, and if you see anything else, you holler."

He starts the Allis moving again, and I watch carefully, imagining myself as an Army scout. The wind picks up a little. About three o'clock I think I see someone in black clothes running beside the trees, but then I decide that it's a shadow caused by the wind moving a bough.

I don't see anything else the rest of the afternoon. Except the grasshoppers.

We have one breakdown, a flat tire on the weed-wiper a little after four. The wiper's three tires are the same size as the Allis's front two, though, and Dad keeps a spare bolted behind the seat. We change the flat and keep working for another three hours.

We show up for supper about a quarter to eight, and Mom's upset because she *told* us she'd have the roast ready at seven. Usually, she wouldn't think anything of Dad's being a little late — breakdowns happen, and things almost always take longer than planned, and she knows that. The only thing I can figure is that she's still mad because of their argument over me.

I'd still be wearing a diaper if she had her way.

Patricia is whining that she wants to go "swim-ming" to-morrow, and Jodi won't shut up about the Walls of Jericho, which was her Bible School lesson today. When I ask her to please be quiet, she takes the red plastic trumpet they gave her and blows it in my face. Dad takes it away and tells her that even Joshua wasn't allowed to blow his horn at the table.

Crissy giggles, although I doubt that she understood a word

79

of it, and burbles mashed potatoes down her front. Mom yanks her out of the high chair and drags her to the bathroom by one arm. The kid starts screaming. I hate it when stuff like that happens at a meal, because then I don't even want to eat anymore.

Dad cleans his plate and gets up from the table.

"Going to wipe some more?" I ask, scooping my corn and potatoes into a pile so I can wolf them down. I figure he'll want to go back to the milo for at least another two hours, working by the bright lights on the Allis.

He puts on his Co-Op hat and shrugs. "I'd better fix that tire first. I won't have time in the morning, and we might need a spare before the day's out. You go ahead and finish your supper, then take care of the calves. Patricia, you can give him a hand."

"You got it," I say.

"Oh, Dad-deee," Patricia whines. "I told Tee-na I'd call her after sup-per."

Dad heads for the back door. "You can still do that if it's not too late after you help with the calves."

"But Dad-deee —"

Dad turns around and comes back to the table. He grabs Patricia by the shoulders and shakes her.

"Not . . . one . . . more . . . God . . . damn . . . word," he says. It scares me a little even though I'm not the one he's mad at.

You better believe Patricia shuts up. If Mom would only crack down on her like that, the brat might actually turn into a decent human being.

Dad goes out to fix the tire, and Jodi sings, "Patti got in trou-ble, Patti got in trou-ble —"

Patricia hits her on the head, and Jodi shrieks.

"Behave out there or you'll wish you had!" Mom yells from the bathroom.

Patricia gets up from her chair, goes behind Jodi, and clamps her left hand over the younger brat's mouth while using her right hand to yank on Jodi's ponytail.

"Stop it," I tell Patricia.

She sneers at me. I get up, go around the table, and pull her hand away from Jodi's mouth. Jodi bellows for Mom.

"That's enough!" Mom yells from the bathroom.

Patricia swings at me, but I block it with my left arm. She's almost two inches taller than me, but I'm older and she's just a girl. If she keeps trying to fight, I'll pound her into the floor.

"I hate you!" she whispers. "I hate you, you little Phillie-baby!"

I walk away from her and get my Co-Op hat from its nail. "Let's feed the calves," I say.

"You're not the boss of me," Patricia says. "You're not the boss of *any*thing!"

I give her the look I've practiced in my mirror, Dad's don't-mess-with-me-now look.

"I'm going to feed the calves," I say. "You can help like Dad said or you can get your butt spanked." And then I head out the door.

She comes out to the barn after I've already filled two buckets with grain. She gives me a dirty look, but then she picks up one of the buckets and lugs it out toward the pen. She looks bowlegged and funny, and I laugh at her.

After taking care of the calves, I find Dad in the east shop. The sun is going down, so he has the lights on inside.

The weed-wiper's tire is one of the old kind, with a tube, and Dad already has it taken apart. He's holding the tube in a rusty fifty-five-gallon barrel half-full of water, and when I come close I see several streams of bubbles breaking at the water's surface as fast as machine-gun fire. A section of the tube as big as one of Dad's hands is riddled with holes.

"What the heck could've done that?" I ask.

Dad doesn't answer me, or even look at me. His eyes are fixed on the froth of exploding bubbles.

"I mean," I say, feeling nervous, "could it've been a knot

of barbed wire?"

Dad lets go of the tube, and it pops to the surface, hissing. Then he turns away and goes to his cluttered workbench, water dripping from his fingers to form a dotted trail on the concrete floor.

"Can you patch it?" I ask.

He wipes his hands on a dirty red shop rag and then takes an old, torn inner tube from one of the hooks above the workbench. He tosses it toward me, and it lands at my feet.

"We'll give it a try," he says. "Cut a patch big enough to cover those holes, plus about a half-inch extra on every side."

I take out my birthday knife, open the second-biggest blade, and sit down on the floor to get to work. While I'm cutting, Dad takes the punctured tube from the water and dries it.

By the time I bring the patch to the workbench, Dad's buffed the rubber around the holes and is brushing on the cement. He takes the patch from me, nods — meaning that I did a good job — and presses it down over the holes with the heel of his right hand. Then he takes two small pieces of scrap lumber, puts one over the patch and the other on the other side of the tube, and clamps the whole mess in the vise on the end of the bench.

"That ought to do it," I say.

Dad looks at his watch and says, "Twenty to ten, Phillie-boy. Better take your bath and read your Bible verses before your Momma comes out and hauls you in by the left ear."

I shuffle backward toward the shop doorway. "You gonna go back out to the milo?" I ask.

Dad is standing by the barrel and looking down at the water, even though there's nothing in it now.

"No," he says, his voice real quiet. "No, I've got some shop work."

"What?" I ask, because I can't think of anything besides the tire.

He looks up from the barrel and frowns at me. "Didn't I tell you to get to the house?" he says, and this time his tone of voice says I'd better hurry.

After my bath, I sit in my pajamas in the living room, and Jodi reads tonight's verses. She has to raise her voice because the box fan is roaring in the doorway, trying to dilute the heat the house has built up over the day.

The verses Mom has Jodi read are the ones about the woman named Rahab who helped the Israelite spies escape from Jericho, and I guess the point must be that if you do a good deed, you'll be rewarded. The spies promised Rahab that the Israelites would spare her and her family if she kept the scarlet escape-cord in the window as a sign, and she followed their instructions. That turned out to be the smart thing to do, because everybody else in the city was slain "with the edge of the sword."

I glance at Mom when the story is almost over. She's looking at the dark picture window instead of at Jodi, which is strange. Usually she's real attentive when we're reading Scripture, so as to correct our pronunciation. When Patricia asks a question about why the Israelites wanted to attack the city in the first place, Mom says something about Communism, then tells us that we've read enough for tonight and had better go to bed.

I use my flashlight to read comics under the covers until my eyes itch, and then I lie awake and listen to night sounds. Frogs are chirruping somewhere close.

After a while, I hear a buzz-buzz-buzzing that isn't like the sound insects make, so I sit up and pull back the curtains from my window. If I peer between two branches of the cedar tree, I can see the east shop from here. Yellow light spills from the shop's doorway into the barnyard, and as I watch, white flashes wash out the yellow for a split second at a time.

Dad is arc-welding something. I lie back and wonder what it could be.

Something to make work more efficient, I'll bet. He's good at stuff like that.

Tuesday. There are no gunshots today, so for a long time

83

nothing interrupts the monotony. After a few hours of riding on the bean-bar, I feel as if the entire world is made of soybeans, weeds, sunlight, and bugs.

Still, the work seems to go faster than it did yesterday, even though the weeds are just as thick. If all goes well, we should be able to finish spraying the beans by early afternoon, or by mid-morning tomorrow at the latest.

Of course, all doesn't go well. Dad likes to quote what he calls Old MacDonald's Corollary to Murphy's Law: "If anything can possibly go wrong, it'll go wrong on a farm." Today, Old MacDonald's Corollary attacks us a little after eleven and clogs up a valve on the sprayer's compressor. Dad tries to fix it, but a hose splits when he reclamps it. So it's a job for the shop, and we have to abandon the soybeans until tomorrow.

But Mom has brought along some grocery sacks, so the morning won't be a total loss. By the time my sisters and I have picked enough gooseberries for a couple of pies, she says, she'll have lunch ready.

That sounds great to me, but naturally, Patricia and Jodi start whining.

"Moh-um," Patricia says, "I'm not wearing any bug spray. I'll get bit-ten. And I'll get poison i-vy, toooo."

"Meeee tooooo," Jodi pouts.

"So go home," I say, disgusted. "I can pick enough for five pies all by myself."

Dad stands up from where he's been squatting beside the compressor and wipes his hands on his jeans. "Take the girls on back to the house," he says to Mom. "I can't mess with this piece of junk until tonight anyway, so I'll help Phillie pick berries until lunchtime."

Crissy is bouncing up and down on the tractor seat. "Me pick! Me pick!" she yelps, spit bubbling at the corners of her mouth.

"You're too little," I tell her, and she glares at me and screams.

So Mom and the two older girls walk back to the house, and

the three-year-old, who will only be in the way, comes with Dad and me to pick gooseberries. She rides on Dad's shoulders, looking down at me triumphantly and chewing on one of her bonnet's ribbons.

I begin sweating the instant we enter the creek's miniature jungle, and I think back to yesterday, when Dad and I found the hunters. I was sweating then, too, but the three trespassers looked cool and calm, as if they were copperheads in human form.

We find a clump of heavily-laden gooseberry bushes surrounding a walnut tree, and I reach in carefully to pluck the marble-sized green fruit while avoiding the prickles. I pop the first berry into my mouth and burst it with my back teeth. The juice that squirts over my tongue is so sour that it makes me shiver.

Dad puts Crissy down beside me, then goes to the other side of the tree to work on a different bush. "Looks like we done struck the Mother Lode, Phillie-boy," he says as he begins to pick.

Crissy reaches for a cluster of berries and immediately gets stuck by the prickles. She shrieks as if she'd just been bitten by a snake.

Dad comes back around and picks her up, then bounces her in his arms until she stops crying. Once that's accomplished, he puts her down again, spreads his handkerchief on the ground several feet away, and tells her to sit on it. She grins and plunks her rump down, more or less on the handkerchief.

Dad and I pick gooseberries, and he whistles a tune he says is from a movie called *The Bridge on the River Kwai*. I've never seen it, but he says he'll let me stay up the next time it comes on. It sounds like fun.

We pick and pick and pick, until the world becomes gooseberries and thorns in the same way that it became beans and weeds earlier this morning. I eat about every tenth berry, and feel as though I'm at the center of a ball of sourness.

Then Dad's hand is on my shoulder, shaking me back to the trees and the heat.

"Where's your sister?" he asks.

I look at the spot where he left her. The handkerchief is still there, but Crissy is gone.

I open my mouth to yell for her, but Dad tells me to stay quiet and listen.

For several long moments I hear nothing but birds, bugs, frogs, and rustling animals. Then, so faintly that I think I might be imagining it, I hear a faraway baby-giggle. Dad takes off running between the bushes and trees.

I leave my sack of gooseberries and follow him, but I can't keep up. After a few seconds I can only see flashes of his blue cotton shirt among the leaves and shadows. He's heading for the creek.

Sweat stings my eyes, and my chest hurts. I'm afraid of stepping on a copperhead, and I wish Crissy had never been born.

At last, I stumble through a clot of weeds and thistles, scratching my arms and face, and find myself standing on a flat, mossy rock on the bank of Coal Creek. Dad is several feet in front of me at the edge of the water, his boots sunk to the eyelets in mud.

Crissy stands in the center of the shallow creek, dark water halfway up her baby-fat thighs. She's grinning proudly and using both hands to hold a broad, shallow straw cone on her head. Her bonnet is gone.

"Daddy!" she yelps in delight. "See Cwissy's hat!"

Dad stands perfectly still, his arms at his sides. I can't see his face.

"Where did you find that?" he asks in a voice that's almost a whisper. It's only because the air is so still that I can hear him at all.

Crissy dances in the water, splashing.

"Pajama man!" she cries.

It's as if the words break a spell. Dad strides toward her, murky waves rippling out before him, and when he reaches her, he yanks the hat away and throws it. It lands upside-down in the water fifteen or twenty feet away.

I expect Crissy to throw a fit, but instead she laughs and claps her hands.

"Boat!" she shouts. "Daddy make a boat!"

The upside-down hat floats lazily downstream. I imagine it going all the way to the Wakarusa river, and from there to the ocean, where it will be eaten by a shark.

Dad grabs Crissy and carries her under his right arm as if she were a bag of grain. When he comes back up the bank with her, I can see his face, and I know it's time to go home.

On our way out to the field, we go by the gooseberry bushes that surround the walnut tree. Dad's sack of berries is gone, and so is mine.

After Mom and the girls leave and we've got the pipewick ready for more weed-wiping, Dad brings out his Remington twelve-gauge pump shotgun from the "off-limits-to-kids" closet in the upstairs hallway. We take it to the milo field with us.

I feel better now that we're away from the house again. During lunch, Crissy kept babbling about "pajama man" and boats, while Dad just stared at his plateful of casserole, He only ate a couple of bites.

All through the meal, Mom watched him with her face set in the expression that means she wants to talk to him but can't because kids are around. She didn't have a chance after lunch, either, because she had to take the girls to town again. All she had time to do was call out, "Be sure to phone the sheriff if those hunters come back," as she was driving the station wagon down the driveway.

Dad didn't answer her. He was already heading toward the east shop to put the patched tire back together.

Now, as we enter the field and begin wiping where we left off yesterday, Dad tells me to keep a lookout again. If I see anything move anywhere, I'm to shout and point.

So I watch, and it isn't long before I see something about a hundred yards away, just south of the bulge of trees where the creek curves.

This time I know it's no shadow, because a broad, conical hat rises above the milo.

"There!" I yell as loud as I can.

Dad stomps the clutch and takes the tractor out of gear, then stands to look where I'm pointing.

The hat rises a little more, and now I see the head and shoulders of the man wearing it. He's too far away for any features to be clear, but I have the impression that his face is leathery. His shirt is of loose black cloth.

"Do you see him?" I yell. "Do you see him?"

Dad reaches for the Remington, which is beside the toolbox, but my legs are in his way. By the time I move and he grabs the shotgun, it's too late. The only things visible between here and the bulge of trees are milo stalks, Johnsongrass weeds, and grasshoppers.

"Fucking bastards!" Dad yells, and his voice is so loud that the tractor engine seems quiet in comparison. I've never heard him use that one word before.

His face is flushed so that it's far redder than his usual sunburn, and veins stand out on his forehead and neck. His hands are clutching the shotgun as if he wants to break it in two.

I don't want him to have to feel the way he does. I hate the God damn fucking trespasser who did this to him.

"You want me to run home and call the sheriff?" I ask. It's the only thing I can think of that might help.

Dad's hands relax a little, and he looks down at me. His face shows his rage, but I know it isn't directed at me.

"You stay right here," he says. "You're my lookout. Hold the gun, and if you see anything else, give it to me."

I know down inside — I *feel* it — that this is the most important thing I've ever had to do.

"You got it," I say, and he gives me the shotgun. It's even heavier than I remember from when he let me shoot it last fall.

I stand on the toolbox and hold the gun. Its stock rests beside my feet on the lid, and its barrel, taller than I am, points at the sky.

Dad puts the tractor in gear again, and we continue killing the weeds that are trying to ruin our crop.

After an hour, we see three more of the men in strange hats and black clothes. Dad spots the first two; I spot the third. They can't be the same person, because they all pop up in different parts of the field within the span of a minute.

Dad fires the Remington at the third even though we're too far away. It seems to do some good, though, because we see no more of them this afternoon.

When we leave the field at seven o'clock, my head is still humming with the vibration of the blast.

As the Allis chugs up the road toward the house, Dad grins at me and pulls the bill of my Co-Op cap down over my eyes. I'm glad he feels better.

"O Lord my God," Patricia reads from the Book of Psalms, "in thee do I put my trust; save me from all them that persecute me, and deliver me . . ."

Patti's trying hard to do a good job, but tonight, again, Mom doesn't have her mind on the reading. Instead, she's staring at the picture window even though there's nothing to see but our reflections. Her fingers are twisting at the hem of her bathrobe as if she's trying to unravel it.

Jodi is sitting in a corner looking unhappy. She's holding Crissy, who is fidgeting and giggling, on her lap.

"Lest he tear my soul like a lion," Patricia continues, "rending it in pieces, while there is none to deliver."

Mom was in a weird mood this evening to begin with, but it got worse when Dad left the supper table without eating a thing.

"Are you sick, Loren?" she asked, and her tone made me want to sink down in my chair.

"Gotta fix the sprayer," Dad said, and went out. I didn't try to go with him, because I hadn't cleaned my plate yet.

Then, when I finally finished my potatoes, Mom told me to go upstairs and straighten my room. As I was going, I heard her tell Patricia and Jodi to do the dishes and look after Crissy.

My room didn't need straightening. I knew that the real reason Mom had given us those jobs was so she could be alone outside with Dad. After a few minutes of rearranging the stuff in my closet, I heard her yelling at him. I had to wait to feed the calves until she was back in the house.

I wish she wouldn't make things so hard.

"O Lord my God," Patricia reads, "if I have done this; if there be in — in —" She looks at Mom.

Mom just keeps on staring at the dark window and twisting the hem of her robe.

I look over Patti's shoulder. "Iniquity," I tell her, pronouncing the word carefully.

Patti looks miserable. Mom told her to read all seventeen verses.

"If there be in-i-qui-ty in my hands," she continues, "if I have rewarded evil unto him that was at peace with me; — yea, I have delivered him that without cause is mine enemy . . ."

There is a clang of metal striking metal outside, from the direction of the east shop, and my muscles jump. Patti's voice falters.

"Pajama man!" Crissy squeals.

"Shhhhhh," Jodi whispers.

Mom doesn't say anything, doesn't move.

"Let the enemy persecute my soul, and take it," Patricia reads. "Yea, let him tread down my life upon the earth, and lay mine honor in the dust."

I think Mom must be the one who's sick. Take tonight's Bible reading — I mean, what does it have to do with anything? Usually she picks a passage about Jesus, or forgiveness, or being grateful, or something like that.

"He made a pit," Patricia reads, sounding confused, "and is fallen into the ditch which he made. . . . His mischief shall return upon his own head, and his violent dealing shall come down upon his own pate."

Crissy giggles. I don't think she understands any of this. I don't think I do, either.

The last verse, at least, is a little more like what I'm used to: "I will praise the Lord according to his righteousness, and will sing praise to the name of the Lord most high."

We all say "Amen."

"Very nice, Patricia," Mom says without looking at her, or at any of us. "You children run along to bed, now, and don't forget your prayers."

In my room, I kneel and pray for God to make Mom feel better. As I finish, I hear the buzz-buzz-buzzing like I did last night, and I look out to see the white flashes.

I was in the east shop after lunch today, but whatever Dad's been welding was covered with a tarp. Maybe, instead of something for the farm, he's making a surprise, like when he made the swingset out of three-inch pipe.

Maybe this time it's a present for Mom, a planter or something. That'd cheer her up, I'll bet.

"Pajama man!" I hear Crissy squeal down the hall.

I'll be glad when she's old enough to know what she's talking about. Then she can let the rest of us in on it.

Wednesday. At breakfast the radio predicted rain for tonight, but the morning is clear and dry. We should be able to finish spraying the bean field today, provided everybody does what they're supposed to. I don't know about Mom, though; she might be too upset to pay attention to the work. I wish there had been some way for Dad to bring the shotgun along without her seeing it. She keeps looking back at it like it's a snake.

Well, like Dad says, we can't very well call the sheriff and ask for a deputy to guard our fields for us. It's our responsibility. So I'm going to keep as sharp an eye out as I can, while still blasting the God damn weeds.

As we move down the rows of beans, the poison spraying from our wands like transparent fans, I can almost see the cockleburs dying. They're sneaky bastards, and they think they can get away with what they're doing by hugging the ground and hiding up against the stems of the bean plants, but we'll teach them better.

I hear Dad shout, and I turn my head to see where he's pointing.

A black-clad, cone-hatted illiterate fool has popped up about twenty rows away. He's so close that I see his rotten-toothed grin before he drops flat again.

Dad stops the Deere, and both Patricia and Jodi fall off their seats.

"Loren!" Mom shrieks. "Dear God, what —"

Dad has brought the shotgun up to his shoulder.

"Did you see where the fucker went, Phillie?" he yells.

"Straight down!"

Dad fires a blast at the spot where the fucker dropped, and a couple of soybean plants are shredded. Bits of torn leaves explode upward.

"Loren, *stop it!*" Mom cries. "You're going to hit one of the children!"

But even as she yells, I see another fucker stand up, closer to the trees. This one is holding a rifle.

"Dad!" I scream, and point.

Dad turns and fires again, but the figure has already vanished.

Mom jumps off her bean-bar seat and runs back to the tractor. She grabs Crissy, who is laughing, and yells at the rest of us kids.

"Philip! Jodi! Patricia! Come quick, we're going home!" Her eyes look wild.

Jodi and Patti go to her, but they move slowly and shakily.

Dad lowers the Remington and squints off toward where the second fucker popped up. "It's all right, Kath. They're gone for now."

Mom grabs Jodi's arm with her free hand and glares up at Dad. "There was *nothing there*, Loren!"

Dad stares at her. "Are you blind? There were two of them, right over —"

"Patricia, Jodi!" Mom says sharply. "Did you see anyone?"

Jodi says "No," and Patricia shakes her head.

My face feels hot. "Then they're blind, too," I say, not caring that I'm sassing Mom.

Mom looks at me, and her expression is one I've never seen before. The only way I can describe it is as love and fear mixed together. I don't like it.

"Philip," she says, her voice quavering, "you're coming home with me this instant."

Dad lays down the shotgun beside the tractor seat. "We've still got beans to spray," he says.

"Philip," Mom says, ignoring Dad, "you get down from that bar and come home *now*."

I don't know what to do for a few seconds, but then I see how unhappy Dad looks. That makes up my mind.

"I can't, Mom," I say. "We've still got beans to spray."

"Philip, you —" Mom begins, but Dad interrupts her.

"You heard the boy," he says.

Mom stands there for a moment, her face puffy and splotched with pink, and then she and the girls walk off across the field.

We watch them until they're on the road. Then Dad sits down on the tractor seat again.

"Women have no eyes," he says.

I raise my spray wand. "Can we do it with just one stream?"

Dad shrugs his shoulders. "We'll do the best we can. We can't do any more."

So we start up again, spraying one row at a time. We see the trespassers five more times, but they stay near the trees, out of shotgun range. Dad fires into the air a couple of times to scare them.

I can't tell whether it does or not.

94

We finish the field and go to the house for lunch at two o'clock. No one else is home, so we make bologna and cheese sandwiches. Fifteen minutes later, we're taking the Allis and pipewick to the milo, once again carrying the shotgun beside the toolbox.

This is the hottest afternoon we've had this week, but there's more wind, so our sweat evaporates fast and keeps us cool. We work for over four hours and don't see any trespassers, so we begin to think that we've finally run them off.

Then we hear two popping noises over the rumble of the tractor. Dad takes the Allis out of gear, idles down the engine, and looks back.

"God fucking damn," he says softly.

Two of the weed-wiper's three tires have burst.

We jump down to investigate, and Dad's Co-Op hat is blown off by a gust. It sails thirty or forty feet, so I run after it while Dad goes back to take a look at the flat tires.

I'm plunging through the milo, planning to yank up the stalk of Johnsongrass that's snagged Dad's hat, when a sharp pain burns up along the outside of my right ankle.

Simultaneously, I hear Dad yell, "Phillie! Stay still!"

But my shoe is caught, and I fall, smashing some milo. My ankle twists.

Dad's here instantly, picking me up.

"I should've known," he says. "God damn it, I should've known."

I look down and see a tight group of at least twenty barbed nails sticking up out of the ground. I've never seen nails quite like them before.

One of the outside nails has stabbed into the edge of my right shoe's sole. Dad borrows my pocketknife and cuts the side of the shoe so I can get my foot out.

A barb has opened a two-inch cut just in front of my heel. It's bleeding, but I can see that it's not bad. My ankle doesn't

95

even hurt much from having twisted.

"Lucky grunt," Dad says.

He scrapes dirt away from the cluster of nails, and I see that they're set into a small piece of board, which in turn is set into a buried chunk of cement. If my foot had landed squarely on the nails so that the barbs had dug in, my momentum would have ripped the bottom of my foot off.

Dad carries me back to the Allis, examining the ground before each step. As we come close to the tractor, I look behind the weed-wiper and see the glint of more nails.

Once we're finally there, Dad climbs up and sets me down on the toolbox. Still standing, he turns to face the trees along Coal Creek.

"All right, Charlie!" he cries. "You fucked with the wrong boy this time!"

Then he sits down, throttles up the Allis, and turns us toward the gate. As we pull out onto the road, I look back and see the weed-wiper wobbling behind us, limping on its flat tires.

Mom is sitting in the kitchen, obviously ready for some kind of showdown. But before she has a chance to say anything, she sees the blood on my shoeless right foot and hustles me into the bathroom, where she makes me sit on the edge of the tub. I hear the kitchen door open and close, which means that Dad's gone back outside.

Mom splashes alcohol onto the cut, and I have to grit my teeth so I don't cry. The sting goes all the way up into my chest.

When it subsides a little, I ask where the girls are. It's hard to keep my voice steady.

Mom begins to clean the wound with a cotton ball. "In town with your Aunt Sue," she says.

"Why?"

She throws the cotton ball into the can under the sink and uncaps a bottle of mercurochrome. "Because."

"That's no answer, Mom," I say, not caring how it sounds.

She tries to give me her don't-back-talk-me look, but she can't hold it. Instead she looks at my ankle and dabs red stuff onto the cut.

"Your father needs help," she says.

The way she says it, like she feels sorry for him, makes me madder than I've ever been.

"I'm all the help he needs," I say. "You just haven't figured it out yet."

Now she looks at me like she feels sorry for *me*, too. "No, honey," she says. "*You* haven't figured it out yet. You're too little."

I stand up. "Are you finished?"

"Yes, honey. Does it sting much?"

"I don't feel a thing," I say, and it's not really a lie, because I'm so mad I can't think of anything else. I head for the bathroom door, planning to get my second-oldest pair of tennies and go back outside.

"You're to stay in your room tonight, Philip," Mom says. "I'll bring you a sandwich in a little bit."

I stop in the bathroom doorway. My impulse is to argue, but I know how much good that'll do. So instead I say, "Yes, ma'am," without looking back, and go on to my room.

Once there, I close the door and put on my tennies and camouflage jacket. Then I pull back the window curtains and peer between the cedar branches toward the east shop.

The Allis is parked just to the west of the building, its front-loader scoop lowered to the ground. The sun is low in the sky, beneath the clouds that are moving in from the south, and the tractor's orange paint glows with the same intensity as the sinking star. The Remington is still in its place beside the toolbox.

As I watch, Mom leaves the house and goes across the barnyard toward the shop. Before she gets there, Dad comes out, pushing a barrel that's sitting in a framework of two-inch angle-iron. The barrel is the same one he used the other night

97

to check the leaky inner tube. It blocks my view of the bottom of the framework, so I can't see the wheels that must be there.

Mom is saying something, but even though my window's open I can't make out her words. Dad ignores her and pushes the barrel over to the gasoline and diesel tanks, where he unhooks the gas tank's nozzle and begins pumping fuel. The barrel must be nearly full by the time he stops.

Then, with Mom still talking — maybe crying a little, too — Dad walks back into the shop and emerges again with a barrel lid and a hammer. Once he has the lid pounded down tight, he pushes the barrel-and-framework contraption into the front-loader scoop. Full of gas, the barrel must weigh hundreds of pounds, but Dad moves it like it was no big deal.

Mom screams now, and I hear every word: "For Christ's sake, Loren, *stop!*"

Dad wipes his hands on his jeans and climbs up to the tractor seat. He starts the engine, and the loader rises, lifting the barrel-and-framework off the ground.

Mom has her face in her hands. I feel embarrassed for her.

Dad puts the Allis into gear, and it rumbles out of the barnyard and down the driveway.

I wait until Mom has come back into the house, and then I take the screen off my window.

Creeping across the sloping kitchen roof is the hard part, because I have to be super quiet. But then I only have to jump a few inches to grab a cedar limb, and from there it's a piece of cake to climb down to the ground.

There's just enough daylight left for me to see the Allis down the road, turning into the bean field. I don't know what Dad's working on tonight, but I'm going to help.

I run down the driveway, bending low in case Mom happens to glance out a window.

By the time I've run across the bean field to where the silent Allis sits, the clouds have moved in and I can hardly see where

I'm going. The trees of Coal Creek are a black mass in front of me. Night insects are whirring and clicking so loudly that I can't hear my own footsteps. I feel lightheaded, worn out.

Dad isn't here.

The front-loader scoop is down, and empty. As I walk around it, I nearly trip over a shallow trough in the soft earth. Dad must have had to drag the barrel from here, so all I have to do is follow the track.

Once I get a few yards into the trees, though, I have trouble. It's so dark that I'm practically blind, and the ground is harder. I can't find any more drag-marks.

But I've got my breath back, so I yell. I get no answer, but Dad has to be in here somewhere.

Something flaps away from the upper branches of the nearest tree, and it startles me. Then, as I'm gathering breath to shout again, I smell something horrible. The stench is just like the one at the low-water bridge two days ago, only stronger, closer.

It chokes me, and I have to let out my breath without yelling. I have the feeling deep in my throat that means I'm about to throw up.

A shrimpy twelve-year-old is little enough use without being sick, too.

So I clench my teeth and force the feeling away, then breathe in deep to try to yell again.

A callused hand clamps over my mouth, but I'm not scared, because I recognize the mingled smells of oil, herbicide, and soap.

"Quiet, God damn it," Dad whispers, so softly that I can barely hear him. "Dead quiet, understand?"

I nod, and he takes his hand away from my mouth. I turn to face him, but all I can see is a dark man-shape. I can just make out something across his chest that must be the shotgun.

He squats so that his head is at the same height as mine. "Is your mother here?" he asks in the same super-quiet voice.

I shake my head, but I'm not sure he can see it, so I whisper,

"She'd be yelling for me if she were."

He's silent for a few moments — listening, I think — and then says, "I'll carry you." He turns, and I get on him piggyback.

Even though the insects become strangely quiet and the brush gets thicker the farther we go, I can hardly hear his footsteps. The sound of my own breathing is much louder.

We come out onto a cowpath, and the stink of the dead thing is worse than ever.

My night vision has improved, but only a little. That's all right with me, because I don't really want to see whatever has died here.

We follow the path for several yards, then cut left and climb a slight rise. As we enter a clump of brush — probably gooseberry bushes — I hear the plop of a frog jumping into the creek.

There's a bare patch of ground at the center of the clump, and Dad stops here, squatting again so I can slide off his back. My tennies crunch dry sticks, and I shudder, afraid of making too much noise.

Dad puts his mouth close to my ear and whispers, "Sit down and be still." Then he's out of the bushes with hardly a rustle.

I do what he says, and I even hold my breath to be quieter. Then I hear a drumlike sound, and I know that Dad has taken the lid off the barrel. A few seconds later, he's back, and I start breathing again.

He lays the shotgun on the ground, then squats in front of me so close that I can see his eyes despite the darkness. He whispers even more softly than before.

"Keep your fingers on this," he says, and guides my left hand behind me to what feels like a strand of monofilament fishing string about three inches off the ground. It's been here all along, tied to the base of one of the bushes, and I didn't even know it.

"What's it for?" I whisper.

Dad starts to chuckle, then stops. "To give ol' Charlie a surprise. When you feel it go tight and then slack, like a one-two punch, you slap me on the arm. All right?"

"You got it," I whisper.

He takes his handkerchief from his back pocket, then reaches under a bush and pulls out what looks like a ketchup bottle. When he unscrews the cap, the smell of gasoline overpowers the dead-animal stink.

He stuffs the handkerchief into the bottleneck.

"What's that for?" I ask.

He grasps my neck with his free hand and squeezes, not quite hard enough to hurt. "Hush. Supply fucked up, so we don't have the mix or igniter. We're improvising." He lets go of my neck, reaches into his shirt pocket, and brings out his butane lighter. "If the trip wire screws up, I'll slap *you*, and you yank on the line. But if one of ours comes through, I'll tell you to cut it. Have your knife ready."

I start to say "You got it," but make myself stay quiet instead. I don't want to fuck up.

Still squatting, Dad turns to face the cowpath. He holds the bottle in his right hand, the lighter in his left. The Remington is beside him on the ground.

I get onto my knees as quietly as I can. The fingertips of my left hand are touching the monofilament line, and my right hand reaches into my back pocket for my knife.

One-handed, I open the biggest blade. Then Dad and I wait.

Chiggers are eating me alive, and I'm afraid of copperheads, but I don't move. I don't even flinch.

I won't let Dad down.

When it happens, I've been here so long that I think I must be asleep and dreaming. I hear soft, weird chattering down on the cowpath, and then the fishing line jerks taut against my fingers.

Almost immediately, it goes slack and drops. I hear a loud

clang and a whooshing sound. My left hand reaches up to slap Dad on the arm, but hits his leg.

He's standing, and the handkerchief in the bottle blazes with fire. It lights his face and gleams in his eyes.

Then he throws, and the flame tumbles over the bushes and down to the path.

As it flies, I think I hear Mom calling me from far away.

A brilliant yellow-and-orange wall leaps up from the path, and my eyes close from the sudden pain of the light. The insides of my eyelids are red, red, red, with dancing bluish-purple flames tumbling across them.

A tremendous roar follows, washing over the distant sound of Mom's voice. I feel as if I've been thrust into the nozzle of an acetylene torch.

"Wienie roast!" Dad shouts. "Gonna have a wieeeeeee-nieeeeee roast!"

I open my eyes and see him leap out through the burning bushes like a ghost. He holds the Remington thrust out in front of him, and he's pumping and firing, pumping and firing, pumping and firing. The blasts are tiny pops punctuating the roar of the world.

The air is full of jumping light.

I look down. My pocketknife has snapped closed over the soft skin between my thumb and forefinger. Blood oozes out over the mother-of-pearl.

Now that I see it, I feel the pain, and it brings me to my feet. The heat of the fire beats at my face, and I start to run through the bushes.

Before I'm free of them, I drop my knife. I stop and get down on my hands and knees to search for it.

"Cook 'em up *hot*!" Dad yells. "Throw 'em in yellow, take 'em out *red*!"

I've lost my knife.

Wanting to cry, I stand and stumble through the crisping weeds. I have to get to Dad.

I find him on the cowpath, flaming trees all around. He's reloading.

The fifty-five gallon barrel is lying on its side not far away, still held at the bottom end by the framework Dad made. The barrel is on fire, the rusty old gray paint hissing and crackling.

I run to Dad, who is raising the Remington to his shoulder again, aiming down the path toward the bean field.

Twenty yards from us, a burning figure is running away. Another comes from the trees to join it, and then another, and another, and they meld together into a single mass of fire.

Dad shoots.

The mass flares, and is gone.

Dad fires the shotgun four more times, then lowers it. His face is dotted with beads of sweat, and they reflect the hundred fires a thousand times. He turns to look down at me, and grins.

His left arm is on fire.

I grab his right wrist. He drops the Remington, but no matter how hard I pull, he just stands and smiles at me.

I feel heat on my legs, and look down to see that my jeans are burning.

Before I can think of what to do, the air is rushing past so quickly that I almost feel cool. And then I'm in Coal Creek, in the mud, and Dad is rolling me onto my side. My face goes under, and I come up coughing.

"You're gonna be okay, Phillie-boy!" Dad shouts.

As I come to a sitting position and look up again, I see that his entire shirt is on fire.

I grab him around his legs, trying to pull him down, but I'm too small. I'm too God damn fucking small.

Dad looks proud and happy.

Thursday. Mom won't leave the hospital, so Aunt Sue volunteers to take care of us kids. That's fine, but I refuse to stay at her house.

She tries to soothe, then argue, and then force me, but I won't listen. Every time she leaves me alone for a moment, I go out the front door and begin walking the twenty-seven miles home. My legs sting, but I don't care.

Eventually, Aunt Sue gives up and takes us where we belong. On the way, she stops at the hospital to tell Mom, who is in a waiting room I can go into.

Mom nods to us, but doesn't say anything.

She wasn't burned, even though she ran into the center of the fire to find us, but she's still in shock. I'm not mad at her anymore, because she was the one who finally pulled Dad into the water, whether she knew what she was doing or not.

"We men," Dad said to me as Mom and I helped him into the front-loader scoop, "we *know* what to do."

It was then, just as I began to feel that everything would be all right, that Mom started crying. I had to push her to make her get into the scoop with him.

Then I drove us home and called the ambulance.

Home. Aunt Sue is bustling about with lunch like a mother hen. She's the take-charge sort, or thinks she is, but with Dad in the hospital, I'm the man of the family. He said so, and nobody can change it.

After lunch, I put on my camouflage jacket and Co-Op hat and go outside.

I fill the Allis's fuel tank, then back the tractor into the east shop and hitch up the chisel-plow. It takes a long time, because I can't manhandle the hitch like Dad can, but I finally manage. While I'm connecting the hydraulic hoses, Aunt Sue comes out and asks me what I think I'm doing.

I tell her what I *know* I'm doing, and if she doesn't like it, she can go back to Topeka.

Patti, Jodi, and Crissy are standing in the barnyard as I'm driving out. They look sad, so I smile and wave. I keep telling them that Dad's going to be okay and that I'll take care of them until he is, but they're still scared and worried.

When I get to the bean field, which is damp from the rain

that came too late, I drive the tractor to the far edge and put it into neutral. Then I dismount and walk into the midst of the blackened trees.

It's a lot brighter in here now than it was with all those leaves and bushes, so I don't have much trouble finding my knife. It's dirty and a little warped, but it's still a damn good knife.

On the way back out, I pat the barrel to hear the booming sound, and my hand comes away smeared with orange-brown and black. All I need is some green to make camouflage paint.

Once I'm in the field again, I don't waste any time. I climb up onto the Allis, lower the chisels, and get to work.

After ten minutes, I see something ahead on the ground and stop the tractor to investigate.

I climb down and stare at the thing for a long time. Despite the smell, I don't feel sick. I kick what's left of the hat, and it crumbles.

Then I take out my knife, bend down, and cut a long strip of scorched black cloth.

As I return to the Allis, I tie the cloth around my Co-Op cap so that the loose ends will blow out behind me. If Charlie comes back, he'll see it, and he'll know what it means.

I settle into my seat, crank up the throttle, and plow the rest under with the burned crop.

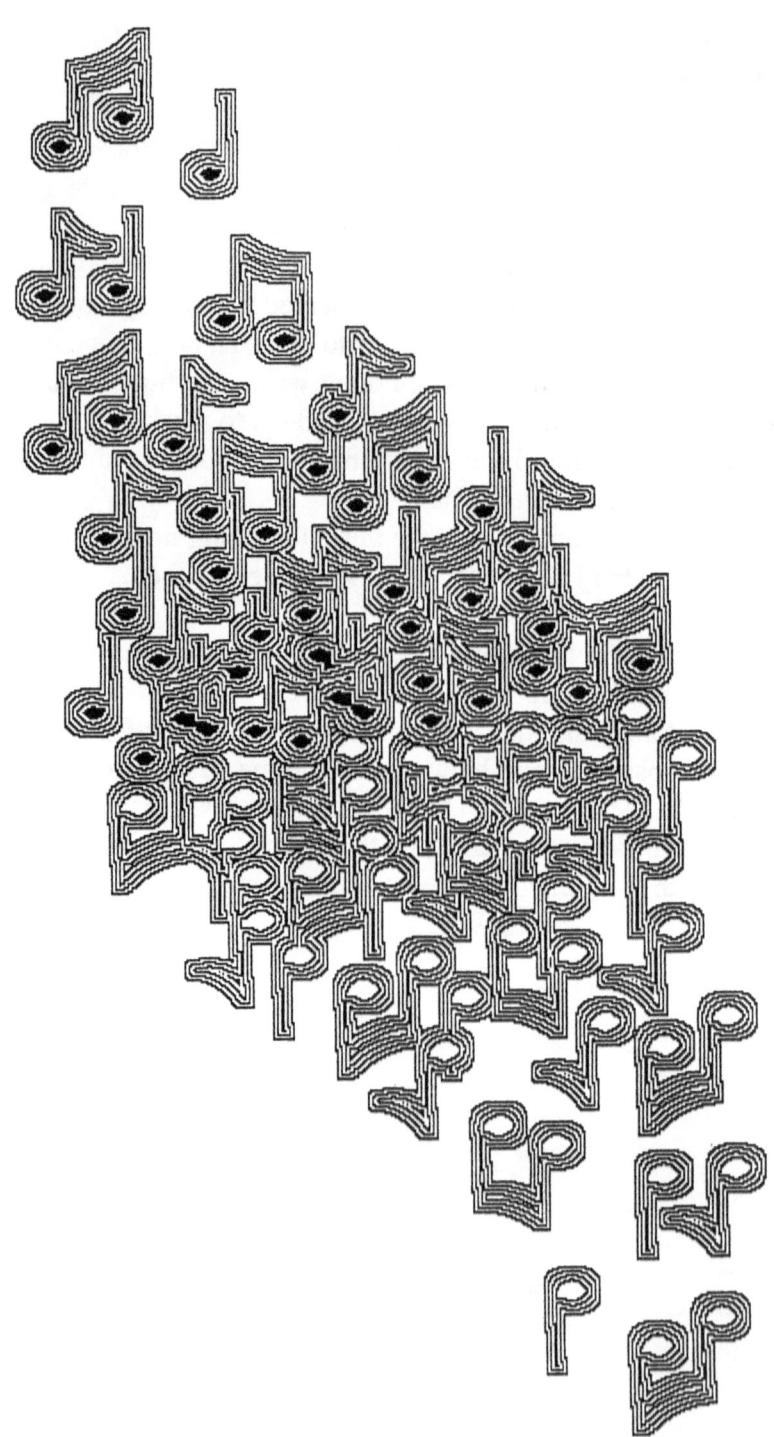

THE MUSIC OF THE SPHERES

"I'm schizophrenic, Lynne," Bobby said as his scan spun out of the printer. It bothered me to hear him say it, because I'd sometimes thought it of him myself. Now, with the possible evidence appearing in bright colors, I wasn't sure I wanted to face it.

Not that it mattered to me if he was somehow different. Bobby was Bobby and always had been. I didn't like the thought of him putting himself through chemical therapy or surgery, so I didn't want him to think that there was anything wrong with him.

The inkjets stopped hissing, and the tractor feed rolled the scan out to where I could tear off the sheet. I smoothed it out on my desk and studied it while Bobby peered over my shoulder.

The frontal lobe did show an abnormal pattern of glucose metabolism; the blotchy, almost surreal blobs of red and yellow clearly didn't correspond to the "normal" positron emission tomography brainscan Rhys and Keller were using as a standard. But neither did it correspond to the standard "schizophrenic" profile.

"You've got an unusual pattern here," I said hesitantly. I didn't want to say anything at all, but I had known Bobby too long to try to get away with silence or a lie. "But it doesn't mean anything's wrong."

That was true enough. The purpose of the study wasn't to identify brain disorders; it was to accumulate enough data from enough different subjects that the term "brain disorder" would take on a more concrete meaning. Even the "normal," "schizophrenic," "manic," and "psychopathic" standards were only guesses in a sense. The people they'd been taken from fit the labels, but nobody could say that the scans absolutely identified them as such. We couldn't be certain, for example, that the pattern identified as "schizophrenic" might not also show up in somebody with a less serious — or completely different — problem.

So the fact that Bobby's scan didn't correspond to the "normal" standard didn't necessarily mean that he was "abnormal." At that stage of the study, all it meant was that his brain chemistry did things differently than the brain chemistry of the person the "normal" scan had been taken from.

But I was bothered by what I saw. I couldn't remember ever seeing a scan look quite the way his did. No two were alike, but there were several basic patterns that recurred over and over again. Bobby's didn't fit any of them. He had read the literature I'd given him, so when he'd seen the odd configuration in the frontal lobe, he'd naturally remembered that schizophrenics tend to have decreased metabolism in that area. But Bobby's scan showed "hot spots" of high activity and streaks and rays that seemed to emanate from those spots. I didn't look at the EEG I'd taken earlier because I didn't want to see if it was just as strange.

For a moment I considered showing the scan to Doctor Rhys, or even Doctor Keller. But it was late, and I was the only one there. The center's official hours had been over long ago, and I'd stayed late to catch up on my work and do Bobby's scan. He couldn't come during the day. If he'd been able to, then maybe Rhys or Keller would've performed the scan and decided that more testing and investigation were needed. I was only the research assistant, though, and I doubted that they'd pay attention to anything I thought was unusual.

Just as well. After all, this was Bobby's brain I was staring at. I didn't want anyone making a guinea pig out of him.

While mildly chiding Bobby for his evaluation of himself, I sealed the hard copy of the scan in clear plastic and labeled it: No. 324, Male, Cauc., 22 yrs. Then I put it into the file cabinet where it would live in limbo until Rhys got to it. Finally, I shut down the scanner, computer, and printer, and gave Bobby his ten bucks.

He smiled his thin, ambiguous smile and asked me if ten bucks was the going rate for schizos. Trying hard to be upbeat, I told him that they usually only got eight. Those who were required to take the technician out for a beer got two extra.

It was lame, but it got us off campus and into a downtown Lawrence bar. Bobby picked it; it was a strange, dark little hole on the second story of an ancient limestone building. I'd never been there before. The place looked and smelled like a cave, and the bare stones of the wall next to our table were cool and damp. It reminded me of the rock shelves by the creek where Bobby and I had played as kids, and I told him so. He said he'd thought of that too.

At first we didn't say much as we drank our beers, but we didn't have to. He knew me well enough to know that I was worried about him. He'd dropped out of school over a year ago and had been supporting himself by bussing tables since then. He was a marvelous pianist, and several of his professors had predicted great things for him. But he'd stopped going to classes, and they'd had no choice but to flunk him. I still didn't know why he'd done it. I wanted to.

After three beers, he said, "Focus. I need to be able to focus myself. That's what I've always needed."

His words caught me by surprise, because I'd been talking about my problems with Peter — small talk, really, just to avoid harassing Bobby about how he was living — and had said nothing that could have logically preceded them. Yet as he spoke he looked at me as if he were answering a question I'd asked.

"Focus," I repeated, stupidly. The taste of beer was mingling with the damp-cave smell and seemed to be drugging me.

He nodded. "I've used you as an excuse for too long. I've been clinging to you ever since I was a kid. But I've got to stop now. You're not my mother. You're not even my sister."

I swallowed more beer and tried to decipher his sentences through the mild buzz in my head. "I might as well be," I think I said then.

He gave me that smile again. "I know. But I can't see you so much from now on. If I do I'll never learn to focus myself."

He had more to say, but I waved my hand awkwardly to stop him. "If I'm going to make any sense out of this," I told him, "you've got to explain what you mean by 'focus.' "

He tried to do that, but he couldn't quite say it so that it was coherent to me. At the time I thought it was the beer doing it.

But whatever he meant by "focus," he felt that he needed to depend on himself more than on me. I was a crutch.

He was careful to add that he couldn't bear the thought of not seeing me at all. He just didn't want to keep on meeting me every day or every other day the way he'd been doing since he'd quit school.

I agreed because it sounded reasonable. He needed to stand on his own a little. And I needed to work on my relationship with Peter.

So we parted that night with a long, hard hug. For the first time in months we didn't set up a specific time to get together again.

I took the long way home on back streets even though I wasn't really too drunk to risk driving the main drags. In fact, I was dead cold sober despite the dull buzz. Bobby wanted to stay away for a while. It had sounded good at the bar, but now I wondered if I'd be able to avoid worrying about him. On the other hand, lately I'd been as worried about my own life as about his.

By the time I got home I'd kicked things around so much that I didn't feel much of anything except tired. All I wanted to do was curl up and sleep.

It was after one when I stepped into the apartment, and I wondered why most of the lights were still on. Peter never stayed up past midnight.

"Lynne, that you?" Peter's voice called from the bedroom.

"Who else?" I said dully. "What're you doing up?"

He stepped out of the bedroom fully dressed, looking at me as if I'd just killed someone.

"You know it's almost two?" he said. "You said you'd be back by eleven."

I shrugged off my jacket and headed for the bathroom. "Sorry," I mumbled. The buzz had become a steady drone that made everything seem as if it were being played to me on a faulty television set.

Peter followed me into the bathroom. Normally I reacted violently to that, but this time I couldn't work up the energy to care.

"You weren't with your little friend, were you?" he said. Accusation and derision mingled in his voice and should have had me up and fighting. Instead, though, I squeezed toothpaste onto my brush and began to methodically scrub my teeth.

"You still claiming nothing's going on?" Peter said.

I spat into the sink. "I've told you a hundred times," I muttered. "He's like a brother. I worry about him. We grew up together. That's all there is to it."

Peter laughed sardonically. "You've been worrying over him until two in the morning? I don't buy it. Not this time."

He paused as if he wanted me to say something, but I kept on brushing my teeth. Somewhere inside, I wondered at myself. Why was I so dull, so unfeeling? Why wasn't I reacting?

Peter sucked in a deep breath, and I looked at him with a feeling of detachment greater than I'd ever experienced before. He was gorgeously attractive — tall, deep-chested, wavy chestnut hair, clear blue eyes — but at that moment he might as well have been a potted plant.

"Lynne, I love you," he said solemnly, "but I'm going to leave if you don't stop seeing this guy. If you want him instead, okay, fine, just say so. But you can't have me too. I've got two suitcases packed and the third one half full. D'you want me to finish or to stay here?"

I spat again and tried to think of something to say. Nothing came.

"You going to stop seeing him or not?" he said.

I rinsed my mouth, spat one last time, and moved around him to the door, unbuttoning my blouse to get ready for bed.

"You hear me, Lynne? You going to stop?"

I walked into the bedroom and shed the rest of my clothes. I knew I should take a shower but decided to wait until morning.

Peter's suitcases were on the bed, so I carried them into the living room before getting into bed and pulling the covers up close around my neck.

"I'm asking one last time," Peter said, standing in the doorway. "Are you going to stop —"

"No," I said.

He turned off the light then and closed the door. I could hear him struggling with his suitcases for a while, and then the front door slammed. A minute or two later his Datsun sputtered underneath my window.

I didn't think I really wanted him to go, but I couldn't work up enough emotion to go down and fight with him or ask him to stay. And I knew that all I would have to do was tell him what Bobby had said about not seeing me so much. He didn't really want to leave — the packed suitcases had been a bluff. But when I hadn't reacted according to script, he'd had to follow through. He was probably cursing himself right now. He wasn't so bad, really; he'd just never learned to control his jealousy.

I listened to the Datsun idle for what must have been ten or fifteen minutes. It was spring, and the thing didn't need to warm up at all. He was waiting for me to come down.

The engine noise finally shifted tone and moved away.

Almost eight months after he'd moved in, Peter was gone.

I found myself thinking that I was the one who was schizophrenic. For a long time it had seemed as if seeing Bobby drained me of all emotion. There was no joy or sadness after being with him, simply a blank. And wasn't that what happened to chronic schizophrenics? Didn't the peaks and valleys of their emotions level out into a constant flat plain no matter what their rational minds wanted them to do or feel?

I turned over onto my right side and saw the rose Peter had brought me the day before silhouetted against the pale white glow from the streetlight. I tried hard to smell it and finally succeeded, but its smell wasn't that of a rose. It was the dustier, more bitter smell of a sunflower like the ones Bobby had brought me when we were kids.

I think he gave me the first one on my eighth birthday. That means he must have been six, in first grade. We were friends because we both lived out of town and our houses were only a quarter mile apart. Neither of us had any brothers or sisters, so that probably had something to do with it, too. Bobby came over a lot since his father liked to work overtime. His mother had died when he was three.

He brought me the flower when he came to wait for the bus with me. "Happy Birthday," he said, and held it out. I took it without any great feeling of gratitude; after all, the southeastern Kansas ditches were full of the things. But I didn't sneer at it either. I was in third grade and Bobby was only in first. He didn't understand things like birthday presents yet. So I pretended to be thrilled and smelled it. He'd picked it on the way, and that August the dirt road was hot and dry even in the early morning. So the sunflower had a coating of dust, and I sneezed. Bobby looked at me quizzically.

I don't remember exactly how it happened, but when we got to school some kid grabbed the sunflower from me and tore off the petals. Without making a sound, Bobby attacked him.

Bobby's face was red and puffy, literally swollen with rage. I'd never seen him look that way before. I was never to see it again.

The kid he was fighting looked the same way.

A teacher would've come out to stop it eventually, but I was afraid that Bobby would be hurt by then. The other kid was a lot bigger. So I dropped my things and leaped into the middle of it, shouting, "Bobby! Stop! It was just a stupid sunflower! Stop!"

When I said "stupid sunflower," he stopped all right. He stopped and looked at me with a blank face. All the rage had vanished in an instant.

And I was filled with the greatest sense of grief that I'd ever felt in my eight-year-old life. I started crying. Life was awful, miserable, and unfair. Nobody cared what you did for them.

In the midst of my misery I was vaguely aware that the other kid was crying too. There was no reason for him to be bawling, though; Bobby had hardly landed a blow. But the other kid's sobs were just as pain-filled as my own.

Bobby didn't cry. He didn't make any noise at all. The rage was gone, but nothing had replaced it. He stood silently, looking at me as if I weren't there.

So when a teacher finally came out, the other kid and I were the ones who were hauled into the office.

On the bus ride home that afternoon, I told Bobby I hadn't meant what I'd said about the sunflower.

Even then he had his strange little smile. I felt a tremendous sense of relief.

"Will you get me another one, please?" I said, and felt even better.

Bobby was the only guest at my birthday party that evening. My mother gave us ice cream and cake, and afterward Bobby and I played the piano in the living room.

Neither of us could really play, but we experimented. His small fingers stretched as far as he could force them. He was

114

trying to create chords.

The sounds he made were eerie and magical, and I felt jealous because he was so much better at it than I was.

He wasn't impressed with himself, though.

"It's not right," he said. "I can't find it."

I didn't know what he meant.

"I can't *find* it," he said again.

He shifted to new keys and tried again. "That's *still* not it." An edge of exasperation had entered his voice.

"Still not what?" I asked, beginning to feel a little exasperated myself.

"The way sunflowers feel," he said.

I was confused.

"You know," he said. "A sound like looking at sunflowers."

He kept on trying. I still didn't know what he meant. But he was only in first grade. He probably didn't know either.

Life wasn't as much fun after Peter left, but it wasn't as much trouble either. I continued to work at the Psychometric Research Center on campus, and I also continued to make halfhearted attempts at getting my master's thesis into some kind of reasonable shape. I even started dating again, a little, but the only men who asked me out were other psych people. Each of them bored me after a few hours, so I started making excuses and finally wasn't seeing anybody at all. It bothered me at first because I'd always seemed to have somebody in the past, but I eventually decided that I could use some time to myself anyway.

And I had it. Bobby had meant what he'd said. For four months after the night of his scan, the only contact I had with him was an occasional hi-how-are-you phone call.

Then, on my birthday, I came home from work and found a slightly wilted sunflower in my mailbox. The note wrapped around the stem was an invitation to hear Bobby play that night.

The address was the bar where I'd last seen him, and that

annoyed me. It wasn't the memory of what had happened that night that was disturbing, though; it was the idea of Bobby wasting his talent in a dingy, damp, moldy place like that. I considered staying home to avoid actually seeing it.

I didn't consider it very seriously. I knew I had to go. I hadn't seen him for a long time, and I hadn't heard him play for longer than that. I needed to know that he was all right and that he hadn't completely given up on himself. I hoped that would be what I'd see.

The place was even darker inside than it had been before. The only lights burning were the dim fluorescent tubes behind the bar and a pale blue haze glowing around a small stage that hadn't been there four months earlier. I could hardly see to walk, and I bumped into chairs and tables and people within a few feet of the door.

That was the first thing that surprised me. I couldn't see any faces, and the hum of conversation was low, but the place was packed with people sitting at dozens of small round tables. The musky odor from their bodies mingled with the sharpness of the alcohol and the dampness of the stone. As I tried to find my way to the bar, I discovered that some were even sitting on the gritty, creaking floor.

My second surprise came when a hand closed around my right biceps and a deep voice murmured into my ear.

"You Lynne Randall?" the voice from the darkness said. "We got a table by the stage for you."

I nodded dumbly and let the hand on my arm pull me through the crowd to a table left of the stage, just out of the blue haze. The table's single chair had somehow remained unoccupied.

"I'll bring you a beer," the voice said as my arm was released. A dark bulk moved away.

The stage was small, and I was close enough that I could have put my feet up on it. It was only about eight inches higher than the main floor.

As my eyes adjusted to the darkness and the dim glow, I saw

my third surprise.

I'd been expecting the usual nightclub-pianist setup, a piano and bench with maybe a mike and small amplifier. But the stage was cluttered with so much equipment that it took me a few minutes to see exactly where the piano was.

Loops of black wire formed dark arcs in the blue light, and huge square shapes hulked at each side of the platform. A jumble of angles and curves surrounded the baby grand at the center, reminding me of unlighted downtown buildings at night.

As I stared, my depth perception failed me, and the whole array on the stage looked like an abstract silhouette cut out of black paper. I closed my eyes to try to reset my optic nerve, and when I opened them again, tiny red lights had begun to burn at random points above the stage. Startled, I moved my hands involuntarily and nearly knocked over the cold glass of beer that had materialized in front of me.

The blue glow intensified slowly, almost imperceptibly, until I could see Bobby sitting at the piano. Even in that weird light, he was unmistakable. His thin body was poised like an acrobat's, and the pale skin of his face and hands radiated a white energy.

A deep, low hum crescendoed with the blue light, and I saw that the shapes surrounding the piano were synthesizers, equalizers, and amplifiers. There was at least one microcomputer keyboard.

My first impression of all this was that Bobby had sold out his talent for electronic gimmickry. But I changed my mind when he started to play.

He began, as he always had when improvising, with a chord. It was played softly, but I could feel it vibrating in my solar plexus. It wasn't just the piano making the sound — Bobby's right hand was at the keyboard of the baby grand, but his left was playing over the keys and switches of one of the synthesizers. It jumped from there to the microcomputer, to another synthesizer, and back to the first. Bobby's body remained tensed before the piano, but his left hand flew around him like a white bird.

Then the chord became a chorus of trumpets, and the sounds from the stage whirled out into the crowded bodies with the force of a maelstrom.

It wasn't volume that made it a soundstorm. It was complexity; it was intensity. It was a rage in the music that throbbed out of the speakers like blood pumping from a burst artery.

I'd never known much about music theory, but I could tell the difference between good and bad. This was good.

A few minutes into the piece, I tore my eyes away from Bobby to see the crowd's reaction. If they had any taste, I was sure they'd be overwhelmed. But I also knew that bargoers generally expected certain things from a musician, and what Bobby was giving them was light years from the usual fare. It wasn't jazz or rock or anything else that could be expected in a downtown bar.

The blue light from the stage was bright enough now that I could see some individual faces. They were more than attentive or appreciative. They were enthralled. The power and rage pulsated in their eyes.

The sound grew louder and the tempo quickened until the music was a turbulent, overwhelming cacophony. Faces twisted, and men and women rose as if the chords pulled them up. I saw fists and bottles raised.

They were going to kill each other.

I snapped my head back toward the stage to scream at Bobby to stop, but my voice was choked off. He was looking at me as he played now.

His face was emotionless. His hands still flew over the keys, but he didn't seem to be aware of them.

I looked back at the people. Most were poised to attack each other, but something held them back. Their bodies swayed as they strained against the tension.

Then the music began to relax and wane, and everyone sat

down again. The piece ended on the same chord on which it had begun, and the audience clapped politely.

I sat numbly. After a long moment I drank half my beer.

The rest of Bobby's pieces that night were played as incredibly as the first, and although the crowd did not become psychotically violent again, their reactions dazed me. When the music wept, so did they. When the music swelled until it was almost sexual in intensity, they moaned. Some approached the stage like impassioned lovers. Once I looked down and saw that a woman was resting her head on the edge of the stage, staring up at Bobby. I didn't know how she'd gotten there; maybe she'd crawled. Tears streaked down the blue skin of her face. The music was too loud for me to hear her voice, but I could see her lips mouthing the same words over and over again: "I love you. I love you. I love you."

Every time I looked up, Bobby was blankly staring toward me.

I didn't know how long the performance lasted, but when it was over, the crowd didn't stay around. They began filtering out of the door even as they applauded.

The woman who had lain with her head on the stage was an exception. She stood at the bar, clutching the edge of the counter as if she would die if she let go.

Bobby flipped a few dozen switches, and all the red lights went out. Then he stepped to the edge of the stage and extended a hand to me.

"Come on," he said.

I let him lead me up over the platform and out a back door that I hadn't seen before.

We stood on a graveled balcony that was really the roof of the store beneath us. A rusty fire escape angled down to the pavement of the public parking lot below. I felt as if I hadn't been breathing for the past hour, so I gulped in a huge lungful of warm August night air. But other than that I felt nothing at all. I was as numb and dulled as I'd been the night Peter had left.

Bobby gave me his odd little half-smile. I caught a brief

glimpse of teeth flashing out of his white, sweating face.

"Well?" he said.

He'd asked me the same thing after every recital of his I'd been to. And as always, I told the truth. "I think you're wonderful. I think I almost see what you meant about focusing yourself."

He looked at me steadily. "I'm beginning to get there. But I haven't made it yet. It's still not quite right."

"The music?"

"No, not really. Me. The music is my channel. I'm trying to focus myself through it." He paused. "And once I've adjusted myself properly, everything else will follow."

I closed my eyes briefly and drew in another deep breath. Bobby's occasional mystical turns had always confused me, so to keep my thoughts straight, I usually tried to think of them in psychological terms. As a result, I'd first wondered if he was schizophrenic almost a decade before. Now I was sure he wasn't, but I didn't know how to explain what I'd seen and what I was hearing. And my emotional flatness made me wonder if my perceptions of things had any bearing at all on what really was.

"I take it back," I murmured, opening my eyes again. "I still don't know what you mean. But I know you're the most powerful musician I've ever heard. And I know that at one point in there I was scared. I've known you all your life, but a few minutes ago you and everything else around me were totally alien."

He touched my hand. "It's only me," he said.

I tried to dredge up enough emotion to smile at him and was able to do it. For him, I was able to.

"It's just that I'm still worried about you," I said.

"I'm fine. Really. What's to worry about?"

I shrugged and tried to treat things lightly. "Oh, all that equipment, for example. How are you going to pay for it?"

He laughed softly. "As of tonight, it's paid for. That's one reason I quit school. Studying textbooks doesn't pay for a Moog."

I heard the door open behind us and looked back. The woman who had cried for Bobby stared out longingly for a few seconds and then disappeared inside again.

"You know her?" I asked.

"Not yet."

We talked for a few more minutes before I kissed him goodbye. Then I went down the fire escape and walked to my car.

In bed that night I kept thinking of Bobby's playing. And I kept seeing the streaked face of the crying woman as she lay in the blue haze.

I didn't know if she had ever seen him before. But I knew that she now loved him with a love she could die for.

I had seen it happen one other time, when I was a senior in high school and Bobby was a sophomore.

We were still close despite the changes that adolescence made inevitable — different friends, different interests, and different reputations. For a while my parents were worried because Bobby was still coming over three or four evenings a week, and my mother even sat down with me one night and told me that she hoped I wouldn't do anything foolish. At first I didn't know what she meant and told her so. When her face grew red, I caught on and had to laugh. Bobby was fifteen and skinny with an acne problem; I was seventeen and had long since realized that I was comfortably although not spectacularly attractive. I was currently dating two of the most popular boys in school, and the fact that Mom was worried about my friendship with *Bobby* was too much to handle with a straight face.

After I stopped laughing, I explained what Bobby was to me as well as I could, and my mother nodded dubiously without saying anything. She still wasn't sure, and I couldn't understand why. Not after all the years Bobby had been my friend.

My father never voiced his own concern to me, but I knew it was different from my mother's. I overheard him telling Mom that he didn't think it was healthy for me to see so much of "a boy who plays piano all the time."

But he was even more wrong about Bobby than she was. One evening in the fall of that year, Bobby told me that he was going to ask Marcia Haines for a date.

I tensed up and bit my lower lip, wondering how I could tell him what I knew I should. Marcia was a senior like me, and she was beautiful. Her mind wasn't much to speak of, but of course that didn't matter. She was tall, blonde, and clear-skinned with long, tanned legs. I was considered "cute," but I knew that if Marcia and I had our eyes on the same guy, I'd better switch mine to someone else. She was head cheerleader and was going with our all-state fullback.

And here was Bobby, pale, fifteen, one hundred and one pounds, telling me that he was going to try to steal her away from the football team.

I didn't want him to suffer the ridicule that I knew was in store. Gently, I tried to tell him that Marcia was stupid, mean, and not at all worthy of him. He just stared at me with no expression.

The next afternoon I saw Bobby and Marcia holding hands between classes. My first thought was that it must be part of some cruel joke she was playing on him, but an hour later I heard the red-faced fullback telling some buddies that he was going to "kill the shrimp."

After school I tried to get to Bobby first to warn him, but the football player had already found him at the edge of the parking lot.

"Y'really ought to come on out for the team," the fullback was telling Bobby earnestly. "I mean it. You're small, but I bet you'd make a good tight end. You can run, I bet."

Bobby laughed lightly and said he'd think about it. The fullback gave him a pat on the back and walked away to practice.

Stunned, I offered Bobby a ride home as usual, but he was going for a drive with Marcia. The last I saw of him that evening was as he was riding off in the passenger seat of her Volkswagen.

Bobby and Marcia were the subjects of incredulous conversations for two weeks, and during that time Bobby didn't come over to my house at all.

Then, on an afternoon two weeks and a day after I'd first seen them holding hands, I found Marcia crying in the girls' restroom.

"He doesn't want me anymore," she sobbed. "I tried to call him last night like I always do and he hung up on me. And he didn't wait for me by the water fountain this morning like he always does."

I searched her face for signs that she was kidding and didn't find any. She was miserable. I said something about going back to the fullback, and she looked at me as if I were crazy. She loved Bobby. Passionately. Forever. But now he didn't want her, and she was going to kill herself.

I didn't believe it. But as I left I thought I saw something metallic in her hand.

I waited a few seconds and then came back just as she was starting to run the razor blade of a utility knife across the inside of her elbow.

My hands clenched the wrist of her knife hand, and I squeezed and pulled as hard as I could while begging her to drop it.

I was stronger and finally won. Her arm had a bleeding cut about a half inch long, but she hadn't hit the big vein.

I threw the utility knife into the trash can, washed Marcia's cut and packed it with a wet paper towel, and then half-dragged her to the nurse's office. I left her there without giving the nurse an explanation; instead, I ran to my class and asked for a library pass. Bobby had a study hall that hour, and he always tried to spend it browsing through the stacks.

I found him and sat down at his table.

"Look at what I'm reading," he whispered before I had a chance to speak. "In ancient times they believed that the universe was constructed of crystal spheres with the earth at the center."

"Bobby, I —"

"And the movements of these spheres created sounds, just like a crystal goblet does. And all the spheres moving at the same time created an incredible chord, a harmony that controlled the universe —"

"Bobby, listen to me." I wanted to work up to it gradually but didn't know how. "I just found Marcia. She tried to kill herself with a razor blade."

He looked up from the book. "Why?" he said.

"Because she thinks you've dumped her. At least that's what she says."

"Oh," he said musingly. "Well, I suppose I have. It was too easy." He shook his head. "I was in love with her a few weeks ago. And then last night I stopped. She called me and I didn't care."

I spoke urgently. "You've got to go to her. Now. Tell her she's too good for you, tell her anything — but she's gone crazy and you've got to stop her before she really does it."

He looked back at his book and closed it slowly. Then he stood. "You're right," he said. "I don't know what I'll do when you move up to the university next year." He paused a moment and rubbed his eyes. "Where is she?"

I told him, and he left the library without asking for a hall pass. He wasn't stopped.

After school, Marcia came up to me in a huff as I was leaving the building. She had a thick white bandage on her arm.

"I want you to know," she said coldly, "that I might have died because of you. There I was, just trimming my cuticles, and you run in as if you're insane. It's a miracle I didn't bleed to death. And what did you do with my knife?"

I think I stood there gaping for several seconds before Marcia's short attention span shifted. "Joey!" she cried. "Oh, Joey, wait up!" And she ran out to where her fullback loitered in the parking lot.

I stared after her, and it was only when Bobby spoke that I realized he was standing next to me.

"Give me a ride?" he asked.

On the way home, I tried to find out what had happened, but all he would — or could — say was that he had explained it to her.

His father worked late that night, so I talked Mom into setting an extra place for supper. And afterwards, as we still always did, we went into the living room to the piano. Now, though, I sat on the couch while Bobby practiced.

"Wouldn't that be wonderful?" he said as he played.

"Wouldn't what be wonderful?"

"The music of the spheres. Music that could rule the whole world, the whole universe. Music that would make the stars and planets spin."

There was nothing I could say. So I just listened.

After the night of my birthday, I didn't see Bobby for nearly six months and heard from him only infrequently. Then, on a Saturday morning in February, a UPS man brought me a flat, square package.

It was a record album. The cover illustration was a blood-red and fire-yellow detail of a solar flare. Above the photograph, in small white letters, were the words "Robert Tallman: *Sunflower*."

I looked at that tableau for a long time before turning over the album to see the back cover. The photo there was identical to the first, but superimposed over it was a list of the pieces included and the instrumentation Bobby had used for each.

At the bottom was something I almost missed.

"For Lynne," it said.

My hands were trembling slightly as I put the black vinyl disc on the turntable. I plugged in headphones to be sure I wouldn't bother the people downstairs.

The album began with the same piece he'd used to start off the set at the bar, and it was all I could do to force myself to listen to it all the way through. I kept seeing the faces of the audience as they surged with the angry sounds.

The other four cuts were things he hadn't played that night. They were all beautiful works, but my favorite was the one that took up the entire second side, the one called "Sunflower." It seemed to me that in most respects Bobby had achieved what he had wanted as a child; the music was alternately dusty and yellow like the flower itself, hot and flaring like the sun, and poignant like the smell I could still call up from my memory.

But for all my pleasure at listening to the complex, intriguing sounds Bobby had created, there was something about all the pieces, even "Sunflower," that troubled me. On an intellectual level, I *knew* that the music was perfect. But emotionally I wanted something more. There was some sound, some chord, that a small, almost unconscious part of me kept straining to hear but that never came.

When I had finished listening, I took off the headphones and began to go about my usual Saturday morning housecleaning chores. One of the first things I did was pick up the cardboard carton the album had come in, and as I was putting it into the trash in the kitchen, a folded slip of white paper fell out.

It was a note from Bobby. He'd bought a house about fifteen miles out of town a few months earlier and wanted me to come visit him now that his "remodeling" was finished — preferably that evening since he had to go on the road the next day.

I went. His new home was a small, white frame house on a two-lane blacktop. The cattle in the pasture across the road blew out their breath in small clouds and watched my car uninterestedly as I turned into the driveway.

Bobby met me at the door and grinned. That startled me, and I couldn't find my voice for a few moments. I had almost never seen him with a facial expression that could actually be called a grin.

"Supper's about ready," he said as I came in. "I wish your mother were up for a visit so I could pay her back for all the

126

times I mooched over at your place."

He wasn't a great cook, but the steaks were high-quality if a bit overdone. I ate ravenously and enjoyed the meal more than any other in years.

The house, at least what I could see of it from the dining room table, wasn't anything unusual. It was old but clean, and the carpet was plain. The walls were a pale blue that seemed too quiet a color for someone who created sounds like Bobby did.

When we'd finished eating, Bobby swept the dishes off the table and brought out the beer. For the next hour we drank and talked about what we'd been doing lately — and reminisced about when we were kids. I didn't have much news to tell; I was still working for Keller and Rhys and their interminable research project and doing little else.

Things had been happening for Bobby, though. Even more things than I'd imagined from the album. I didn't listen to the radio much, so I hadn't known that *Sunflower* was already getting more airplay than any other album in the nation, even though it wouldn't be in the record stores for another week. And Bobby was leaving the following afternoon for a twelve-week concert tour. No band and only a few roadies. It was his show. He was more successful than I could have dreamed.

Yet here he was sitting across the table from me, drinking a beer, still Bobby, still thin, still pale, still my little brother.

"You want to see my studio?" he asked after we'd finished off a six-pack.

"Sure, sometime," I said, thinking that he was talking about some operation in New York or Los Angeles.

Smiling, he gestured for me to follow him and took me through the kitchen to a white door beside the refrigerator. He opened it, and I followed him down into the cellar.

We stepped through a second door at the bottom of the stairs. His finger touched a switch, and I was in a different world from that of the plain blue walls above.

127

Brilliant white light flooded a chamber that looked as if it belonged in a starship. White acoustic baffles covered the walls and ceiling, and the gray floor felt like rubber. Black amplifiers and speakers towered in the corners and hung from the ceiling on silver chains.

The room was tiered like a tiny coliseum, and each tier had its own array of black and silver wires and equipment. At the center, in the pit, the keyboards of the piano, synthesizers, and computer, ringed a small gray space where I knew Bobby would stand.

Part of one wall was a large pane of plexiglass behind which I could see the outlines of big multitrack tape machines in a tiny booth.

"You go in there," Bobby said, pointing to it. "The door's just to the right of the window. It's a little hard to see." I must have looked uncertain, because he grinned again to reassure me. "It's the best place to listen. You can talk to me by pushing the button on the chair arm."

After a few seconds of fumbling, I found the door handle between two baffles and let myself into the cubicle. I closed the door behind me, settled into the single chair, and looked out at Bobby.

The bright white light from the studio had made it possible for me to see the chair, but the control console was a black field below the window. I wondered if Bobby could even see my face in the dark booth. As he flipped switches and plugged in wires, small blue lights began to glow in front of me like hot stars.

"What would you like to hear?" he asked when he'd finished with the switches. His voice came from the walls and ceiling of the booth, and I felt as though I were in the center of an enormous amplifier.

My first impulse was to request "Sunflower," but I'd heard it twice that morning. So instead I asked him to play something new, something he had just composed or was still working on. I wanted to see what he would do to top what he'd already accomplished.

His right hand reached toward a metallic band atop one of the synthesizers but then drew back awkwardly. He started to mumble something about not having anything new, and I stopped him by thumbing the button on the chair.

"You can't lie to me," I said. "You've never been able to. So tell me what that thing is."

He hesitated for another moment and then picked up the band. As he gingerly fitted it over his head, I saw that thin, silvery wires attached to it led to a black box interfaced with a microcomputer.

"The headband," Bobby said quietly while looking down, "contains electrodes to pick up my electroencephalic signals — alpha waves in particular. The computer interprets the currents and uses them as control signals for three of the synthesizers. But the program's not quite right yet. I haven't got the filtering perfected. And I haven't yet been able to control my alpha waves as well as I want to. I'm hoping to work out the bugs on the tour."

"Sounds like you're breaking new ground," I said, trying to be encouraging. "I want to hear it."

He adjusted the headband and looked toward me. I couldn't tell if he could actually see me or not. "In some ways," he said, "this isn't new at all. Performers were using electroencephalic currents as control signals for electronic instruments as early as 1965. But I'm hoping to take things a little further and use this to help me . . ."

His voice trailed off as he flipped more switches and adjusted dials and knobs. He didn't need to finish, though. I remembered what he'd said months earlier. It wasn't the music that he wanted to perfect. He wanted to use the music to perfect himself. To help him find his focus.

He began to play. His hands moved slowly and somberly over the keyboards, and I was surrounded with the sound of a storm building over a funeral. Then, as I watched him, his eyes closed, and his forehead tensed.

And a clear, high fluting pierced through the boiling black clouds, shoving them aside to make way for sunlight.

It was quite pretty. Yet there still seemed to be something absent . . .

The music rose and whirled and spun. The funeral became a wedding, and then a revel, and then a white light exploded behind my eyes.

It couldn't have lasted more than a few milliseconds, because my brain didn't even have time to assign a name to the experience. But whatever had been missing was there in that instant. It struck me full force and tore the soul from my body.

It was wonderful.

And then it was gone, and I was on the floor. Bobby was trying to lift me up. I thought he might be crying.

"I'm okay," I tried to say, but I couldn't hear my voice.

It was several minutes before I regained any control over my body, but eventually I was able to help Bobby get me into the chair. He held my face in his hands and watched me anxiously.

"Bobby," I mumbled. "You look like you're feeling something."

"I tried to tell you," he whispered. "I knew the filters weren't under control yet. But I wanted to play for you anyway. I wanted to. I'm sorry."

I flexed my fingers. Everything seemed to be working now. "What was it?" I said. My voice was strong again.

Bobby's facial expression began to relax back into its more characteristic blankness. "Filtering problem," he said simply. "It got too loud."

I was about to question him further but stopped myself. I didn't want to force him into an outright lie. "Loudness" in the usual sense had nothing to do with what I'd felt. My ears weren't hurting or buzzing. Nothing in the booth had vibrated or broken.

Maybe, to Bobby, "it" had indeed gotten too "loud." But that wasn't the right word for me.

I struggled to find the right word and couldn't do it. It had happened too quickly. But I knew it was what had been lacking in "Sunflower" and the others.

He'd turned on the lights in the booth, and I was able to see his eyes clearly. If I tried, I thought, I might be able to find my answer there.

He looked back at me without flinching. His face was smooth and blank, but his eyes were concerned. They didn't waver from mine.

I found no answer, not in his conscious solicitude. His music was on another level, something more basic, more important . . .

"Maybe I'd better play for you another time," Bobby said. His half-smile was back.

"Good idea," I said, standing. I was a little surprised to discover that my legs weren't shaky. "Your amplifiers pump a few more watts than I can handle."

He glanced away and nodded slightly.

"Got any more beer?" I asked after a few seconds of silence.

Bobby shut down his equipment, and we went back upstairs. It was only when we had entered the kitchen that I recognized the smell of the studio by its absence: ozone. I remembered smelling it as a child after a thunderbolt had split a tree in our front yard.

After a few more hours I was a little too tired and drunk to drive home, so I spent the night on the couch in Bobby's living room.

I usually don't remember my dreams, but that night I had two that were especially vivid. In the first I had a lover whose face was always obscured by darkness, but I could see his head because of the silver band of light that encircled the featureless oval. It was as if his face were the sun and couldn't be looked upon, and so the moon eclipsed it, leaving only a silver corona.

In the second dream, a pale face with dark lips and eyebrows hovered over me like a vampire in an old movie. Then it came down and kissed me once on the forehead. When it drew away, I was outside my body and saw that the kiss had left a red mark like a wound. As I watched, a thick stem sprouted from the mark and grew into a flower with a dark center and golden spikes for petals.

I woke up then — at least, I thought I was awake. I shifted position on the couch, and as I did so I could just see Bobby's bedroom door closing in the darkness.

He left the next day, and I knew I wouldn't see him again for twelve weeks. The final concert of the tour was going to be in Kansas City in the big sports arena by the stockyards, and he gave me a ticket for the main floor and a backstage pass. By then, he said, he would have the "filtering" for his new instrumentation perfected.

So for three months I found myself waiting for the day when I would drive into Kansas City to hear him again. When I realized that I was living only for that day, I almost hated myself. I had turned my life into a cycle of seeing Bobby and waiting to see Bobby. It was stupid, really, I thought. I wasn't responsible for him and didn't have to think about him constantly. I had my own life, and my work was important.

I tried to concentrate on that and couldn't. I kept remembering things that had happened when we were kids, the night at the bar when I'd first heard his electronic music, and the nameless stab I'd felt in his studio. All that stayed with me, even when I was doing my job at the research center.

Especially then. Less than a week after Bobby left for the tour, Rhys pulled his scan from the file. I came in on Thursday morning and found her and Keller arguing over it.

Both of them specialized in the relationships between brain physiology and psychology, but their opinions on specifics differed wildly. Keller had done considerable research into what he called "extrasensory phenomena" and had an unshakable belief that telepathy not only existed but had a physiologi-

132

cal basis. Rhys, however, thought that humans were lucky if they were able to break out of their own skulls enough to communicate verbally. As a result, I'd always felt more comfortable with her than with Keller. She seemed to have a firmer grasp of reality.

As I listened to them argue, though, I found myself being more sympathetic toward Keller.

"If this individual were dangerous, as you suggest," Keller was saying, stabbing a finger at the laminated hard copy of Bobby's scan, "he would not have been available for a reading. He would have been incarcerated long ago."

Rhys shook her head firmly. "I'm merely stating the obvious: his brain displays an abnormality of a type we haven't encountered before. So it's important that he be studied further to determine if he's harmful to himself or others. Especially in light of the EEG."

Keller snorted. "You're relying on your study of alpha wave patterns — what was it, fourteen years ago?"

I winced at that. Rhys would defend her research to the death.

Her back stiffened noticeably. "That study has been supported by others around the world. It's virtually a proven fact that criminals, as a group, display a high degree of slow alpha wave activity."

"Perhaps so," Keller said, raising his finger and waving it vigorously. "But are you certain that sculptors or policemen or musicians don't display the same trait? Have you checked?"

Rhys pressed her thin lips together for a moment before speaking again. "All I've suggested is that this person displays both an EEG and a PET scan that are abnormal enough to warrant further testing."

"You also said he might be dangerous. That's what I take exception to. Why, this might even be the natural telepath I've been looking for . . ."

"Always the same fantasy," Rhys muttered.

Keller was about to retort, but I coughed to announce my

presence. They hadn't noticed me yet, although I'd been in the room for several minutes.

"Ah, there you are, Lynne," Rhys said. She picked up the scan and walked toward me. "Neither of us remember taking this, and it's unusual enough that I think we'd recall it if we'd done it. I realize you've processed nearly twelve hundred subjects by now, but if you could examine this and perhaps . . ."

I knew whose scan it was before even seeing it.

So should I tell them or not? I wondered.

I pretended to study it carefully. "Interesting," I said. "But we've been telling our subjects that their scans are confidential."

"Of course. We're not considering revealing his name to the public. Do you remember the subject?"

Rhys and Keller were both experts, and, whatever their disagreements, they both saw something strange in Bobby's scan. If Keller was right, there'd be no harm in further testing, and it might even be worthwhile. And if Rhys was right, this would probably be my last chance to do anything about it. Bobby was going to be exposed to at least a million stomping, shouting people throughout the coming weeks, and anything might happen to him or to others if his brain went haywire.

Maybe it would be best if I told them. Maybe Bobby needed help.

Maybe . . .

"No," I said, and shrugged. "No, I'm sorry. There've been so many. And this was —" I pretended to squint at the date in the corner. "— nearly a year ago."

Rhys nodded grimly, as if that was what she had expected, and took the scan back from me. I was, after all, only a graduate student, and not an exceptionally brilliant one at that. I could hardly be expected to remember one out of hundreds.

She and Keller argued for a few more hours, but then the subject dropped and wasn't brought up again. Neither of them had been all that concerned after all, I told myself. It was just an excuse to disagree with each other.

But I *had* noticed the strangeness of the scan when I'd taken it. I'd noticed because it was Bobby's.

And because it was Bobby's, I wouldn't tell anyone.

Maybe that was wrong. I didn't know.

And I didn't care.

From the outside, the arena looked like a huge, white, bloated creature. I couldn't shake the image, and it was reinforced when I had to breathe the dirty, smoky atmosphere inside and hear the deafening murmur of twenty thousand tightly packed human beings. It was a murmur of potential danger and power, and it was waiting for something — a signal. The mob was a single entity, and it wanted a thing that could not be named.

Whatever the thing was, it was embodied in Bobby. When the massive floodlights hanging from the distant ceiling blacked out and a single white spot of brilliance illuminated the figure on the stage, tiny amid the black angles of his equipment, the breath of the mob exploded in a roar of thanksgiving.

It began just as it had the previous August, and I had to leave my seat. I couldn't stand being in the midst of that rage, that barely restrained frenzy. The screams of excitement had changed to cries of anger and terror.

I began walking up the aisle, and then running. By the time I stopped I was near the roof of the arena, far away from the stage.

From that vantage point, Bobby seemed to be a miniature automaton surrounded by flesh, and I saw how his music controlled the living mass. It pulsed out in ripples, and the ripples spread through the thousands of bodies as if they were water.

The single white spotlight stayed on him, and he moved only slightly as he played. Silver flashed from his forehead. He was wearing the headband.

When the anger subsided and was transmuted into something

else, I began to walk slowly back to my seat.

The people I saw as I walked were crying, laughing, and hugging each other. They sang along with the wordless music as if words didn't matter. Only the sounds mattered; only their raw voices had meaning. They made love without touching each other.

No: by touching in ways they had never touched before.

Sweating, drained, exhausted, I slumped into my seat and gazed up at Bobby. He was looking at me. He knew where I was.

He was playing the song he had tried to play for me at his house. It was the song of breaking through rage, through pain, through death, just as the sun broke through clouds. Everyone around me felt it. Their joy consumed them. They had never known it before. They reached for Bobby and sang their love for him.

All around me, they were being transformed.

And I was untouched.

The music was beautiful. I knew that. But he was playing something else that I couldn't hear.

Everyone else heard it. I could see it in their bodies' movements, in their slick, happy faces.

And realizing that I was alone, that I couldn't feel what they felt, I forced myself to feel nothing. Even that was better than aching. For the first time, I was aware of the effort it took.

It went on for three hours. I sat there listening to the music while the others lived in it. Once I wanted to leap up and scream *Why? Why them and not me? Why?*

But I knew — I knew in my forever rational, forever reasonable mind — that the asking would hurt as much as the answer would. So I beat down the thing rising in my throat and sat quietly while the people around me intertwined like threads or tongues.

When it was over, no one moved for the exits. They all stayed seated, reclined as if basking in a delicious afterglow.

I looked at the stage, and Bobby was gone. I hadn't even seen him leave.

There was no encore, and no one shouted for one. After several minutes people began to stand and mill around, talking to each other and laughing as if they were at a gigantic family reunion.

I stood too, and I made my way toward the right side of the stage where I'd noticed barricades earlier. I had a backstage pass. I wanted to get to Bobby, grab him by the shoulders, and shake him until I knew what was wrong with me.

The burly black man at the barricade smiled and only glanced at my pass. I was about to walk through the opening he made for me when I felt a touch on my shoulder.

It was Peter. I hardly recognized him at first in the dim light, and when I did the first thing that came to mind was that he'd left just over a year ago. I hadn't seen him since.

When he spoke, his voice didn't sound like anyone I'd ever known. He was changed, elevated. He wasn't the Peter I'd lived with.

"I'm glad I found you," he told me, smiling. "Before you say anything, I've got to tell you I'm sorry. I'm sorry for the way I was. I know I don't deserve to be forgiven, but it's important to me that you know I'm . . . sorry." His irises flickered strangely.

I must have said something, but I didn't know what it was.

Peter's eyes turned toward the unknown area beyond the barricade. "You see," he said. "I didn't know then. I didn't know why you kept seeing him. Now I do."

Something in my chest churned. Peter knew something, yes; but it was nothing even remotely similar to anything that I'd ever known.

He continued to stare toward the backstage darkness. "I know how you must have felt then," he said. "How you must feel now." He looked down at me for a brief instant. "You're awfully lucky," he whispered.

137

Then he kissed me on the cheek and turned back into the crowd.

When I found Bobby, he wasn't surrounded by the throng of admirers, guards, and lovers I'd expected. He was alone, sitting on a black trunk.

He grinned. "I've been waiting for you," he said.

I could only look at him.

His grin melted away. "Lynne? Something wrong?"

Again, for an instant, I wanted to scream my question. And again I squelched it. If there was an answer, I could find it myself. Quietly. Rationally. Without emotion. Without screaming.

Maybe I already knew it.

"No," I said, and I felt my facial muscles turn my mouth up into a smile.

"Good," Bobby said, grinning again. He got off the trunk and hugged me. "Well? Am I a success?"

"You're a success," I said.

He laughed. It was a clear, high note, almost like singing. I'd heard him play many times, but I'd never heard him use his voice to sing before.

He released me from the hug, and I saw sparks in his eyes.

"You've reached it, haven't you?" I said slowly.

He nodded.

"I suppose, then," I said, "you'll be leaving music for other things."

"Soon. Changes are coming."

I bit my lower lip and looked down at the floor. Streaks of gray dust scarred the dark surface.

"You going to bother me anymore?" I said, trying to joke.

"Always," he said. "Not too often from now on. But I'm an incurable moocher." He paused. I didn't look up to see if he had any expression. "Infrequently. Rarely, even. But you'll never be completely rid of me."

He opened the trunk then, and I was able to feel something when I saw he'd brought the beer.

The Music of the Spheres was delivered to me two weeks later. It consists of cuts that were recorded on the concert tour. I still haven't taken off the plastic.

Bobby dropped out of sight after the tour, and the critics and fans have been lamenting their loss for the last three months. Just two days ago I read a feature in the Sunday paper that speculated about what might have happened to him. In the course of her research, the reporter had found Bobby's father and interviewed him. But the only thing he could say was "How the hell should I know?" They were never close, despite the fact that they were the whole family. Bobby's dad never understood the piano playing any more than my father did.

After reading the article, I drove out to Bobby's house on impulse. It's empty now, although I think he might still own it. I wonder if the studio's still in the cellar.

I've decided to stop working on my thesis, and I'm only doing my job at the center out of habit. It's not that I'm giving up; it's just that everything I've learned and everything that Rhys and Keller have been trying to learn won't mean much before long. I don't think so, anyway.

Everybody saw it: Today on national television, beamed by satellite to every country on earth, the President of the United States and the President of the Soviet Union began sobbing as they met for strategic arms negotiations. And then crying outright. And then they hugged like two bears and swore that they loved each other as brothers.

No one has criticized them. Not *Pravda*, not the Pentagon, not Congress, not the local chapter of the John Birch Society. No one.

The news commentators cried too.

I'm tired, but I can't sleep yet. The clear plastic on the album cover peels off in thin strips, like Christmas tinsel.

No, Doctor Keller. That scan wasn't your long-sought-after natural telepath. Telepaths only deal with thoughts, with our rational minds. They can't affect the lower layer, the one of passion, of hatred, of love. They can't make us feel simply by feeling themselves.

He loves me. He loved me. Past, present, always. When he was six years old. When he dropped out of college.

In most ways, he's always loved everyone else, too. But he never had any reservations about making them feel it in return.

Me, though — me, he wouldn't force. He filtered me out, left me untouched.

Bobby, didn't you know I'd be glad for it, glad to know the name of what I felt in your studio?

The hum in my ears tells me that the volume is probably turned up too high, but that's all right. I want no distractions now.

None except the smell and feel of the flowering weed I found in my mailbox today. Happy Birthday.

The first crystalline notes blast into me like ecstasy, and I close my eyes, trying to fill in the missing chord.

THE SUMMER WE SAW DIANA

Falling in love with Diana would have been redundant. That was the kind of person she was. That's the kind of people we still are. None of the others could stop, even if I told them about the oscilloscope.

There must be a better way to begin. Where should I start? And to whom should I speak?

If I were Joseph Conrad, I could create a Marlow to tell the story of our summer. He'd have four listeners on the deck of a yawl, and they would discover a whole truth they had only glimpsed before. To Marlow, you see, the meaning would not be "inside like a kernel" but "outside, enveloping the tale which brought it out only as a glow brings out a haze . . ."

But I must be my own Marlow, my own Kurtz, my own Intended. And a glimpse of truth has already done enough damage to my potential listeners. They can't see the haze.

So while waiting for Shelby to return from another job interview, I whisper to my warped reflection in the beer pitcher as if it were my secret sharer. For the deck of my yawl I have the Intersection, where it began. " 'And this also,' said Marlow suddenly, 'has been one of the dark places on the earth.' "

The college town of Oread, Kansas is one of those known beyond the earth.

I was drinking at the bar the first time Diana came in. It was a Saturday afternoon in a humid April, and most of the regulars were here: Jack Tyler, who was working at the plastic cup factory; Shelby Stevens, then about to get her clinical psych degree; Ed Burke and his girlfriend Laura; Bill Sandwich-and-Tea; Thad Harris; a few others. We all looked up when Diana entered.

She wasn't beautiful in her Army-surplus pants and blue flannel shirt. But something about her caught and held our attention — a slight asymmetry of her greenish eyes, maybe, or the pendular motion of the dark blonde braid that hung to her knees. Or the smile she gave each of us.

As she sat down beside me and ordered a draught, the scent of honeysuckle replaced the Intersection's usual sour-dusty smell. Ronnie, the owner, was bartending, and he poured ten or twelve ounces of beer on the floor before getting the glass under the tap.

Diana looked around at the decaying gray interior. "I've been in Oread since January," she said, "but this is the first time I've noticed this place." Her voice was like the high notes of a cello.

I leaned close so we could talk without shouting over the Grateful Dead coming from the stereo behind the bar.

"It's popular with old hippies and others who never finish anything," I said, extending my hand. "I'm Lawrence Dillon, professional student. Everybody calls me Larry."

"Diana Chandler," she said, and put her hand in mine. An electric tingle told me she was my kind of person.

"Nice to meet you," I said, wanting to hug her.

" 'Larry' isn't right," she said. "Could I call you Lawrence?"

How had she known that I secretly liked my real name?

My turn was over quickly that evening. First Ronnie leaned over the bar to shake her hand, and then Thad sat down with us. Shelby came up to make sure Diana didn't think we were hitting on her. Jack approached and offered to marry her. And so on.

The only one who didn't like her was Ed's girlfriend Laura. When Diana held out her hand, Laura pretended not to see. I decided I'd never liked Ed's taste in women.

When I left, most of the others were still enjoying themselves. It was especially good to see Bill Sandwich-and-Tea laughing, because he'd been awfully quiet lately. Shelby thought he'd tried to open his wrists a few years back, and we were afraid he was considering it again.

But now that Diana was here, he seemed to be all right.

I was ashamed to discover that I felt jealous. A part of me already wanted her all to myself.

But Diana would never belong to any one of us. We had to share her, or we'd lose her.

I didn't know that the first night. But I was to be the only one who ever really understood. I was to be the one who lost her for all of us.

The Intersection was closed Sunday, and Monday I had to attend two graduate seminars and teach a composition class. I finally made it in a little after five, dying to see if Diana would be back.

She wasn't, but a few of the others were. Shelby sat beside me at the bar and bought us a pitcher.

"Whattaya think, Dillon?" she said, brushing her dark bangs from her forehead and putting on her gun-moll act. "We gonna start foolin' around again?"

I made myself smile, then looked at the wet rings on the bartop. Shelby didn't try so hard to be funny unless she was dead serious underneath.

"Well?" she said, making a sound like snapping gum.

I took a sip of beer. It tasted flat. "Dunno, Shel," I said. "I thought you had a thing going with that prof who tortures monkeys."

She dropped the act. " 'Had' is right. He cares more about the monkeys than he does me, and he sticks things in their brains."

I remembered the time she'd given me a tour of the prof's

143

lab. I hadn't learned exactly what the project's purpose was, but it had something to do with inducing certain types of behavior by electrically stimulating appropriate brain regions.

What had struck me most about the place, besides the smell, was the contrast between the animals and the machines connected to them. In one corner had been a cage where a macaque with a wire in its skull had masturbated; next to it had been a table with a small glowing screen and a graph printer. The monkey had hooted frantically, and the printer's needle had calmly scratched a jagged red trail.

The research was probably important. But all the same, as I sat in the Intersection with Shelby, I was glad the monkey prof was through with her.

She took the pitcher and topped off her glass, then said, "I guess I feel inadequate, what with him dumping me and everybody here nuts for that Diana chick."

I became defensive. "Nobody's nuts for her. She seems to be a loving person, and we're drawn to that."

Shelby leaned to whisper in my ear. "Speaking of which, Bill went home with her Saturday night."

Bill Sandwich-and-Tea was the most asexual person I'd ever known. "I don't believe it," I said.

Shelby made a snorting noise. "Because it wasn't you?"

I was about to ask what the hell she meant when Bill came in and headed toward us. He sat down beside Shelby.

"Sandwich and tea, Ronnie," Bill said, and Ronnie went into the kitchen.

"How's it going, Bill?" Shelby asked, grinning.

Bill grinned back. "Just great." He looked at me. "You left too early the other night, Larry. We had a good time. Didn't we, Shel?"

"Not as good as you had later, I'll bet," she said, waggling her eyebrows.

"Jesus, Shelby," I hissed.

Bill laughed. "That's okay. Everyone knows."

I took a pull at my beer and set the glass down hard.

Shelby put a cool hand on my arm. "Easy," she said softly. She could be that way — caustic or funny one instant, comforting or calming the next. I hated it.

Bill looked troubled. "Is . . . something wrong?" he asked hesitantly.

"No," I said, and refilled my glass.

Shelby took her hand away. "Larry's afraid that his rep as town stud is in trouble."

I smoldered.

Bill watched me with concern in his eyes, and it made me nervous. It was as if our roles had reversed. "Larry," he said, "I'd never do anything to make you feel bad."

"I don't feel bad," I lied.

"I hope not," Bill said. "But if you do, well . . . I needed her." His face was red. "It might not happen again, and it's okay if it doesn't. But she made me happy."

There was such wonder in his voice that I couldn't respond. It was as if he'd been reborn.

Shelby's face held an expression that probably matched mine. She hadn't expected anything like this either.

Ronnie brought Bill's usual ham and Swiss with an iced tea, and Bill ate as if savoring the food of the gods.

Diana came in about an hour later, and some of the others swarmed around her as if she were the Messiah.

It bugged me. I began to wonder whether I liked her so much after all.

Until my turn. When she sat with me and touched my hand, I loved her again. I even forgave her for sleeping with Bill instead of me.

We became addicted. The Intersection hours weren't enough, especially since Diana had "a Wednesday night class" that formed a black hole in the middle of our week. So we began meeting at her apartment after closing.

I loved being at Diana's. She only had a studio apartment, but we were always comfortable. And there was always the chance I might get to stay the night. Always the chance, I told myself.

In most respects, she lived simply. Her bed was a mattress in one corner of the room, and several large pillows served as furniture. Her kitchen appliances were a tiny refrigerator and a hotplate. The only wall decoration was a poster of Einstein riding a bicycle.

In contrast to all that was a few thousand dollars' worth of electronics. She had a tuner, an amplifier, a cassette deck, a turntable, an oscilloscope, an equalizer, and a forty-channel citizens' band radio all stacked on brick-and-board shelves between a couple of big speakers. But her record and tape collection was small, and she didn't often play anything when we were over. Sometimes she put on quiet background music, but that was all.

My guess was that an admirer had given her a lot of stuff she didn't really have a use for. It seemed a waste, so one night I had Ronnie bring over some of his albums so we could see what the Dead looked like on the oscilloscope.

But Diana herself was what I was most interested in, just like everyone else. Except Laura, who never came to the apartment. Ed felt torn, but I didn't worry about him.

I worried about Shelby. Throughout May she ate too many caffeine pills and studied almost constantly. I was glad when she finally took off the Tuesday night before exams started and came to Diana's with the rest of us. I was even more glad when she and Diana had a long talk. Shelby needed a friend with more patience than I had when she invariably got around to discussing psychology. As I left, she was telling Diana that behaviorism was inhumane and that B.F. Skinner was a sonofabitch.

I chuckled and closed the door. Shelby'd been a devout behaviorist when she'd been sleeping with the monkey prof.

The next afternoon I went into the Intersection and saw her

sitting alone in a corner. I got a beer and went over.

She didn't raise her eyes or speak when I sat down, so I knew something was wrong. Shelby could be warm, nasty, loving, or violent, but she was never merely silent.

I drank my beer and tried not to stare at her.

After twenty minutes or so, she said something I couldn't hear. I had to ask her to repeat it.

"I said," she murmured, "I'm afraid I'm a lesbian."

I didn't know what I'd expected, but that wasn't it. "Oh," I said stupidly.

She looked up at me. The whites around her dark brown irises were bloodshot.

"I'm serious," she said. "I slept with Diana."

A quick pang shot from my stomach into my chest.

It was jealousy.

"Well," I said carefully, "that's no big deal."

Shelby gave me one of her "Thanks a lot, jerk" looks.

"Really," I said. "One, uh, experience doesn't . . ." I wanted to run out and bury myself in a muddy ditch.

"I liked it," she said.

Then I was angry. "Congratulations," I said sardonically.

She looked as if I'd stabbed her in the heart.

What happened was that she came home with me.

We'd had a brief affair before she'd taken up with the monkey prof, and it had been nothing more than two friends having fun. But now we made love desperately, as if trying to prove something.

When we finished, Shelby said, "That was nice."

"But not great?"

"I said it was nice, and it was."

So how was it with Diana? I almost asked. Not to be mean, but because I wanted to know.

We lay on our backs. A breeze from the open window blew across us, and Shelby pulled the sheet over herself.

"God damn," she said.

147

"What?"

"I've got a final in the morning. I should be home studying so I can graduate with honors and get a job. Instead I'm lying in your bed wondering if I'm gay."

I got under the sheet and pressed my face into her right shoulder. I tasted salt.

"Don't," I said into her skin. "Maybe you're bisexual. Maybe you're an asexual who's faking all the way around. But don't *worry* about it."

"Easy for you to say, you male Caucasian heterosexual shit."

I rolled onto my back again and tried to change the subject. "What's tomorrow's exam?"

She was silent for a moment and then giggled. " 'The Psychology of Sex,' " she said, and convulsed.

We exhausted ourselves laughing.

It was a moonlit night. When I was finally able to turn toward Shelby again, her body was a smooth, damp shadow with an arc of ivory at the hip.

"What were you thinking about?" she said later.

"When?"

"When your eyes were closed."

My fingers twisted a few strands of moist hair. "You closed yours for a while, too," I said. "Were you thinking about anything?"

"No. Just enjoying you."

"Me too."

She laced her fingers behind my head and put her mouth close to my ear.

"We're lying." She whispered so softly that I thought I might be dreaming it. "We were both thinking of Diana."

Toward morning we made love again. This time I kept my eyes closed the whole time. Shelby must have too.

It was wonderful.

148

Exams were over by the end of May. Diana was still unavailable on Wednesdays, now because she had to "babysit" for somebody. I was out of a job since classes were over, but I'd won a small grant to do a research paper on "Heart of Darkness" and "The Secret Sharer" that would get me through the summer.

The days were hot, the Intersection's beer was cold, and we all loved Diana.

Sometimes I wondered what her power was. No other woman had been to bed with Thad Harris, who was gay and glad of it. No other woman had made Shelby think she might be gay herself. No other woman had made me want her so much that I was afraid of both of us.

It had something to do with the intensity of her gaze, the openness of her love . . .

When you talked with Diana, you and she were the only people in the world. I didn't know how she did it, but I had seen it at work. And I had felt it.

But Ed's girlfriend had not. On the first Saturday in June, the day before the accident, I heard Laura say something while Ed was in the Intersection's restroom. She muttered "slut" when Diana walked in and sat at a table with Bill, Jack, and Shelby.

I was standing beside Laura at the bar, and my back stiffened. "You say something?" I asked, keeping my voice at a level only she could hear.

She shook her head.

"Yes, you did," I said.

Laura looked exasperated. "Christ, Larry. I know she's a sacred cow, but all I see is a hollow little whore who tells you all exactly what you want to hear. And screws like she was in heat."

For an instant I was stunned. Then I imagined hitting Laura in the face, bloodying her mouth.

I gripped the edge of the bar. It felt slick and hot.

"You incredible bitch," I said. My jaws were clenched so

149

tightly I thought my teeth might break.

Ed's voice behind me said, "What's that?"

He came around to stand beside Laura, and he looked at me with a strange expression.

Laura put her hand on Ed's arm and smiled. "Larry was just saying that life's a bitch."

Ed frowned. Then he said, "Ain't it the truth," and gestured to Ronnie.

He knew what I had really said. I was pretty sure he was beginning to agree with me.

The tension broke a little when Jack came over and invited us to go sailing at the reservoir the next day. He'd already talked to Shelby, Bill, Thad, and Ronnie, and they were all going. So was Diana.

Ed and I said we'd be there. Laura didn't say anything, but she'd be going since Ed was. She'd want to be sure he and Diana weren't together too much.

After Jack went back to his table, Laura asked Ed to take her home. As usual, he paid the tab for both of them.

"Whores charge," I said to the air while Ed was at the cash register at the far end of the bar.

I could feel Laura's eyes on me, and I had to look.

There was no hatred in her face, but there was anger and pain.

"Watch out for the ones that don't tell you the price ahead of time," she said, and glanced at the table where Diana was holding Bill's hand.

As Ed and Laura left, I wanted to take the heavy glass pitcher from the bar beside me and heave it at the back of Laura's head. My fingers even closed on the handle.

Then Diana came over and touched those fingers, and I felt nothing but love and peace.

Sunday morning was bright. The lake shimmered.

We wondered if it was safe for all nine of us to pile onto Jack's eighteen-foot catamaran. But there was a life jacket for everyone, and Diana, who was holding Jack's hand, said we'd be fine since there was almost no wind.

That settled us. No one wanted to stay on shore when Diana was going to be on the boat.

A nylon-seated aluminum "wing" extended from each hull, so six of us sat on the wings while the remaining three stayed on the canvas between the hulls. Shifting people around when we tacked was difficult, but on the whole there was plenty of room. We enjoyed ourselves for three hours.

Then Laura noticed the greenish-black clouds in the southwest.

She pointed them out to Jack, who looked irritated. But with a thirty-foot aluminum mast over us, he admitted, we didn't want to get caught in a thunderstorm.

The nearest place we could land the boat was a mile due south. The waves whitecapped before we'd gone halfway, and then the clouds were over us. It began to hail.

"Tacking!" Jack yelled, and those of us on the canvas ducked as the boom jerked from port to starboard. Marble-sized hailstones rattled on the boat and stung our skin.

Laura shouted something I couldn't hear over the noise of the storm. She was on the starboard wing, clinging to Ed as though she would die if she let go.

Cold water washed over us. Thad fell into the lake.

A violent gust whipped the boom back to port. It hit Jack in the head, and he pitched into the gray water.

As he disappeared, I looked at Diana. She sat on the bucking port wing as if carved from white ice. Her eyes were open wide, and she didn't even wince as the hailstones struck her.

Several of us grabbed at the swinging boom, but there were too many trying to do the same thing at the same time. The boat lurched, and we went overboard.

I came up about twenty feet away and saw a spike of light jump from the mast into the sky.

Diana was the only one still on the catamaran.

What I saw in that instant I was sure I dreamed. Diana's eyes glowed red, then green, then diamond blue. Her hair whipped around her like charged wires. White fire blazed from her mouth.

Then the concussion hit like a giant hammer, and the sailboat flipped over.

I tried to scream Diana's name, but my mouth filled with water. I choked and spat, then swam hard for the capsized boat.

A cold terror told me she was already dead.

As if at a command, the hail and wind stopped. The waves began to subside.

I saw Jack bobbing a few yards away from me. His right ear was bloody, but he was conscious.

"Where's Diana?" he shouted.

"She was still aboard when the lightning hit!" I cried.

Jack looked confused and scared. "Lightning?"

"Didn't you feel the thunder?"

"Jesus God," Shelby's voice said a few feet to my right. I hadn't known she was there.

I turned toward her, and then I saw it.

Less than a quarter mile away, a thin, dark funnel licked down from the clouds. As I watched, it touched the water and turned white.

I made for the boat again. Peripherally, I saw Jack, Shelby, and somebody else doing the same thing.

It was pointless. Even as I swam, I could feel myself being drawn backwards.

Then I was enveloped in mist, and a current pulled me under. For several long seconds I felt as though I were encased in black ice.

When I surfaced, the funnel was retracting into its cloud mass. But the storm wasn't through with us.

I don't know how it happened; maybe a shelf of rock twisted the currents created by the waterspout. But however it had been created, a whirlpool at least twenty yards in diameter and seven

to ten yards deep drew me in and carried me along its upper edge.

The catamaran was at the bottom. The mast rose up every third or fourth turn and sliced back into the water like a knife into soft wax. The mainsail and jib were gone.

Through the mist, I saw the others. Four were near the top of the whirlpool, like me, and the rest were lower. But only Diana was with the boat.

The boom ropes were tangled around her legs, and she was being dragged along as the boat spun. Her head and shoulders were underwater almost constantly.

I tried to go to her, but the whirlpool wouldn't let me move downward any faster than it would take me. I thought I might have better luck if I took off my life jacket, but then I looked across and saw that Jack had already tried it. Now he clung tightly to his unstrapped jacket, and I instinctively checked the buckles on mine.

I heard a shout above the water-noise.

It was Laura. She was farther down than anyone but Diana, and she was pointing at the body. I couldn't hear all she said, but I picked out the words "She's drowning!"

I tried to shout back that it was too late, that Diana had been hit by lightning before going into the water, but Laura didn't hear me.

She grabbed a trailing rope and pulled herself toward the boat.

Her thin arms held more strength than I could have imagined. She went down across the current until she was within three yards of Diana's entangled foot.

Then the mast came out of the gray wall and swung down. It caught Laura across the back and drove her under.

She didn't come up.

The water slowed. In fifteen minutes, the center of the whirlpool was no more than a dimple where the boat turned lazily.

Diana's perfect shoulders rose from the foam. She floated face up.

We circled with the gentle current and watched the one we loved open her eyes.

It took the divers three days to find Laura. The funeral was two days after that. It was a week later that Ed Burke slept with Diana for the first time. A Friday.

And that was why, as I tried to feel sorrow in the weeks following Laura's death, all I really felt was jealousy.

I had to remind myself that Diana loved me as much as anyone. She belonged to all of us, and I could live with that. As could the others.

Except Ed. After that Friday, he kept her hand in his at the Intersection. Whenever others sat with them, he glared and sulked.

For him, making love with Diana hadn't been the freeing experience it had been for Bill. Instead, he had seen it as meaning that she would take Laura's place.

She did spend extra time with him for a while. But by mid-July she was returning to her old patterns, and Ed began to realize he was no more important to her than anyone else.

He couldn't accept it. He had to be the center of her universe, as he had been for Laura.

On a Wednesday evening in late July, I sat with Shelby in the Intersection and told her what I saw happening, hoping she would know how to prevent the coming crisis. But when Ed came in, I knew it was too late.

His hair was greasy and tangled, and his face was covered with dark stubble. His eyes were wide and watery.

"Anyone seen that bastard Jack?" he shouted. "And where's Ronnie?" His lips pulled back from his teeth. "The son of a bitch waited until I went home!"

Ronnie was in the kitchen, but none of us said so. Ed pushed Thad out of his way, went behind the bar, and slammed a pitcher down on the Grateful Dead album that was playing on the turntable.

Ronnie came out, and Ed swung the pitcher into his right temple. Ronnie spun and fell.

"You were with her Sunday!" Ed screamed, and raised the pitcher again.

I ran and landed with my chest on the bartop, then reached up and grabbed Ed's wrist. He lost his grip, and the pitcher smashed on the floor.

I rolled away as he struck at me. Then I saw that Jack had come in.

Ed jumped over the bar and got his hands on Jack's throat.

"You killed Laura!" he shrieked. "I won't let you take Diana too!"

Shelby pulled at his arm, and he elbowed her in the ribs. But he let go of Jack.

I got Ed in a bear hug. Jack leaned on a pinball machine and coughed.

"You've been with her!" Ed cried, struggling. "I saw your car! And now she won't answer the door!"

"Ed, this is Wednesday," Shelby said. "She's not home on Wednesdays."

Ed began screaming incoherently.

Then Thad's voice boomed, "Call an ambulance!"

That distracted me, and Ed stomped on my right foot. Even before the pain hit, he had twisted free.

Jack dodged away, but Ed didn't notice. He kicked over a table and stumbled out of the Intersection.

Bill Sandwich-and-Tea came out of the restroom. "Hey," he said mildly, "what's all the noise?"

"Ed went crazy," Jack said hoarsely.

I limped toward the door. "We'd better go after him before he gets hurt."

Shelby stopped me. "We have to help Ronnie," she said.

Ed, her eyes told me, was past any help we could offer.

At the hospital, the police asked how Ronnie had been hurt. There was no way to avoid telling them about Ed.

I wish we had done it sooner.

Shelby, Jack, Thad, Bill, and I had been in a hallway about two hours, waiting to hear about Ronnie, when they brought Ed in.

They took him right past us. Blood got on Shelby's purse on the floor.

Jack began making soft sounds in his throat, and he and Shelby cried. Bill wandered down the hall. Thad swore.

I went outside to get away from the odor of antiseptic. It was a hot night, and clouds of insects formed halos around the lights shining down on the parking lot.

A policewoman leaned with her elbows on a metal railing, smoking a cigarette and muttering.

"Goddamn crazy," she said. "Stupid, stupid."

I asked if she knew what had happened to Ed.

Apparently, he had wandered around Oread on foot after leaving the Intersection. Wandered around and walked through windows and glass doors.

The policewoman had found him at the last place, after he'd fallen. His last words before losing consciousness had been "Diana. I saw you."

"You knew him?" the cop asked.

I nodded.

"Okay, then," she said. "Who's Diana? Some girl who dumped him?"

"I don't know," I said.

The cop looked at me skeptically and then turned away to puff on her cigarette. She exhaled smoke and said, "The doctors don't think he was doped up, but we still ought to question this Diana."

"Why?"

She stubbed out the cigarette on the railing. "To find out why he did it."

157

"I doubt that he knows that himself."

The cop looked at me again. "Wrong tense. They gave up on him a few minutes ago."

I went back inside and told the others.

After another hour, a doctor said that Ronnie had a concussion and would have to stay a few days. We could visit him the next afternoon.

Thad and Bill left with Jack. I rode with Shelby, and she drove as though driving were the most important thing in the world. I knew it kept her focused away from what wanted to eat her alive from the inside out.

"Stay with me tonight?" she asked at a stoplight without looking at me. Her eyes searched the intersection.

I couldn't answer because of what I kept thinking.

"Somebody has to tell her," I said.

The light turned green, and Shelby accelerated slowly. "It's Wednesday," she said. "She's not home."

"It's not Wednesday anymore. It's at least one o'clock. Let's go."

"No," Shelby said.

"Why not?"

She pulled over to the curb.

"Because I need her now," she said. "That's what happened to Ed. He needed her too much."

"You can wait outside."

"I won't. You'll stay with her."

I put my left hand over her right. She was clutching the steering wheel so tightly that her knuckles felt sharp. "I've wanted to before," I said, "and I haven't."

"This time you'll need her. And you'll stay."

A car went by, and its headlights showed me that Shelby needed to cry but was stopping herself. She took us back into the street and drove to Diana's.

I rang the buzzer for several minutes and was about to give

up when the hallway's single bulb burned out. Only then did I see the flickering at the bottom of Diana's door.

Pale green licked out and made my shoes look phosphorescent.

I pressed my ear against the door. Something inside hissed.

I told myself it was the sound of leaking gas. If I had believed it, I would've kicked in the door. Instead I fumbled in my wallet for a credit card and used it to pop the latch.

There was no stink of gas as I entered the room and closed the door behind me. The only smell I was aware of at first was the pleasant, sweet scent of Diana.

Then I saw that the green light came from the oscilloscope, and I smelled something intermingled with the sweetness. Something like warm plastic and metal, like a television or computer.

For a long moment all I could see were the green waves and spikes that danced across the circular oscilloscope screen. Then my eyes adjusted, and I saw Diana's silhouette. She was sitting cross-legged on the floor beside the shelves of stereo equipment.

I took two steps toward her, then stopped as another weak light came into view.

The red numerals had been hidden by her body, but now I saw that the CB radio was monitoring channel thirty-one. The hissing sound had been static.

But there was no sound now. The line on the oscilloscope danced in silence.

I took another step, and the line went flat. The CB emitted static. Diana did not move.

The room was cool, but I was sweating. I felt as though I were in a dream.

"Diana?" I said, and the static stopped. The green line jumped again.

My first thought, like a dream-thought, was that the static and the glowing line were connected to my actions. I took another step. Nothing changed. "Ed died tonight," I said, and still nothing changed. The line rippled, and Diana sat as if frozen.

Just as she had during the storm.

Fire had come from her eyes and mouth. Fire like the white of the lightning, the green of the oscilloscope, the red of the CB's channel indicator, and the blue of —

I shook my head to get away from dream-thought. There was no blue.

I went to Diana and knelt beside her. "It's Lawrence," I whispered.

Green washed over the left half of her face, leaving the right in shadow. Her left eye stared.

"Why are you like this?" I asked. "Did Ed —"

Static hissed and startled me. That sound, I realized, meant that the radio was in the receiving mode. I looked away from Diana for a moment and saw that the oscilloscope displayed a flat line again.

I took Diana's cold face in my hands and turned it so I could see both eyes. She didn't seem to feel me.

I ran my hands down her neck and shoulders, then grasped her upper arms and shook her.

She was an ice sculpture.

"Diana," I whispered. "Please. I need you."

My fingers slid down the thin cloth covering her arms. I needed our hands to touch as they had so many times in the Intersection. I needed to know she was still our Diana.

Then I felt the plastic-coated wires. They entered the back of each of her hands behind the knuckles of the middle and ring fingers.

I stared at the twin green lines reflected in her eyes as my fingers probed. Ed and Laura were dead, Ronnie was in the hospital, and the woman I loved, the woman we all loved, had wires in her.

Wires.

160

I thought of the monkey prof.

The static cut off abruptly, and the lines in Diana's eyes resumed their dance.

I brought her right hand close to my face.

A flap of skin was peeled back, and two strands the thickness of fishing line disappeared inside, where tiny blue lights gleamed.

When the static came back, the blue lights winked out. I looked at her left hand and saw that they were there now.

I traced the wires from Diana's right hand and found that they plugged into the oscilloscope. Other wires led from the oscilloscope to the CB, and two wires led from there to the left hand.

A rational demon worked without my will and told me that when the green line danced, the oscilloscope was taking signals from the right hand and feeding them to the silent, transmitting CB. When the line was flat and the CB emitted static, the left hand was receiving signals from elsewhere.

I remembered the masturbating monkey and the machines that had recorded its brain's feeble energies.

And I ripped the wires out of Diana. Sparks jumped from the holes.

Her eyes burned red, green, and blue. A white flame shot from her mouth.

Then the room was dark and silent. The oscilloscope and CB lights had gone out.

The smell of plastic and metal lingered.

I groped at the wall until I found the light switch. The dusty globe on the ceiling gave off a dull yellow glow.

Diana lay on her back, her eyes closed. I propped up her head and shoulders with a pillow, then knelt and watched her. I couldn't think of anything except the lab and its monkeys, and my memory of the stench began to overpower the realtime smells of Diana and her equipment.

161

She opened her eyes and smiled.

"Lawrence," she said in the clear voice I loved.

I touched the skin behind her knuckles and felt no seams. Her hands were warm.

"We've waited so long," she said.

Her left hand touched my cheeks and lips, then stroked my hair.

I met her open mouth and tasted honeysuckle.

She undressed us. Her touch was unerring and loving, her mouth soft and sure. The fingers of her right hand intertwined with those of my left.

"You hurt," she breathed. "When you hurt you don't know what's right or wrong, real or unreal. Let me take away the hurt."

They were words I needed to hear, and I nearly cried out as I moved toward joy.

She touched me as I wished, let me touch her as I wanted, combined words and flesh in a perfect, delicious —

The rational demon stirred and sent me a thought like a stab of lightning into a storm-whipped lake:

No reality could be so like my fantasies. There is always imperfection, in anything, in everything . . .

As I kissed Diana's throat and breasts, I realized that her right hand still clasped my left.

She whispered, "I won't let go of you. Not now. Not ever."

I pressed my mouth against her skin and tried to melt into her.

The demon's lightning returned:

Again she has said and done precisely what I wanted, precisely what would erase my fear.

"We've become one," she said, sliding her left hand down my spine.

It was good, it was real . . .

The honeysuckle went away for an instant.

A hundredth of a second. Less.

My tongue tasted warm plastic and metal.

I tore my mouth away, put my right hand on her breastbone, and tried to push free.

Her right hand kept my left imprisoned.

I got to my feet and pried at her fingers.

"Lawrence," she said. "I am you."

She reached up with her free hand and touched me.

Almost, I let myself have what I wanted.

Then the demon ripped through my desire. I stumbled backward into the wall and leaned there half-crying as pain throbbed up my arm.

My left hand was paralyzed, claw-like, as Diana had held it. Bits of bloodless skin were caught in the fingernails.

"So it must end," a clear, sweet voice said. "It'll be good to be in my own body again."

I looked from my hand to Diana.

Naked, she knelt on the floor in front of me, her hands palm-down on her thighs. Ragged tears marred her right hand, and a blue spark flashed inside.

The perfect woman, the goddess, stood. My right hand reached for her again.

She ignored it. "I meant to stay longer for the sake of completeness," she said, "but I'm told my data has been sufficient." She went to the shelves of equipment. As she stooped to retrieve the wires, she glanced at me. "I suppose you'll go mad now. You're all so close."

I didn't feel as though I were going mad. I had been on the brink of joy and had pulled away. There was nothing left to feel.

But the rational demon was not dead. "That's what happened to Ed, isn't it?" my voice asked. "He was here tonight and saw you."

Diana plugged wires into her right hand. "He left just as I became aware of him. When I'm in contact, I can't pay much attention to anything else. That's why I scheduled my reports at weekly intervals. If nothing else, you tend to respect your clocks and calendars."

163

If I had been able to feel, I would've felt anger. "He loved you," I said.

She plugged wires into her left hand and shook her head. "My findings are clear. Except for rare individuals, you respond only to behavior keyed to your own wishes. You 'love' only what serves you. Surprisingly little progress has been made since the last survey."

I began to feel something now: a dizzying confusion, as if I were being drawn into a cold whirlpool. "When was that?"

Diana flipped switches on the oscilloscope and CB. "It can't matter to you."

"It matters," I said, not knowing why.

Diana sat cross-legged and looked at me with an expression that was almost pity. "A few dozen of your lifetimes ago."

My left hand twitched, and the rest of my body shuddered in response.

"Why here?" I murmured. "Why us?"

She adjusted one of the wires in her right hand. "Yours was only one of the groups in this sample. If it's any consolation, no other group has fared much better than yours." She seemed to hesitate. "Or much worse."

I walked toward her and heard blood squeezing through the vessels in my head like static, like hissing.

"I'll tell them," I said, kneeling before her.

"For what purpose? Besides, by the time you can say anything, I'll be gone."

Her left index finger paused over a button on the oscilloscope.

She gave me the smile that had made us love her. It was tinged with something we hadn't seen the first time.

"I'm sad for you, Lawrence," the cello-voice said. "If you were capable of truly loving me and mine, we'd be more than willing to love you as well."

Her finger touched the button, and her arm dropped to her side. The whirlpool roared.

I wanted to shout my hate, but no sound would come from my mouth. I wanted to rip out the wires again, but my hands wouldn't move.

I don't know how long I looked into her empty eyes. The sun was up by the time I found myself standing on the sidewalk outside. My left hand was sore but unparalyzed. I had managed to dress myself. I managed to walk away.

That afternoon I was told that Bill, Thad, and Jack had gone to Diana's at 8:00 AM to tell her about Ed. The apartment door had been open, and there had been nothing inside but the poster of Einstein and his bicycle.

The Grateful Dead are singing their last songs of the evening, and it's time to make an end.

Again, if I were Conrad, I'd conclude with a perfect metaphor. I'd have my Marlow and his listeners look out from the deck of the yawl and see that "the tranquil waterway leading to the uttermost ends of the earth flowed somber under an overcast sky — seemed to lead into the heart of an immense darkness." Or, if I felt optimistic, I'd have my narrator see his secret sharer, his second self, transformed into "a free man, a proud swimmer striking out for a new destiny."

But the ends of the earth are both too far and too near for our story. Oread is only a tiny piece of the earth, yet it's played a part in the judgment of the whole. As for a new destiny — how can I describe a self as "a proud swimmer" when it's struggling to float?

I know it's poor tale-telling to invoke another's stories. But I've clung to my Conrad research as Shelby clung to her steering wheel the night Ed died, as a man in a whirlpool clings to his life jacket. Besides, my funhouse pitcher-image, although I've drained your gold and left you with foam-flecks, you're an indulgent listener. You don't require me to judge as Conrad required Kurtz to judge. We won't whisper of "the horror."

Still, a storyteller has a duty, and I don't want to fail you. If

165

I were a classicist, I might now portray Laura as Cassandra, whose prophecies were true but never believed. Or Ed as Actaeon, who was changed into a stag and torn apart by his own hounds after he saw a naked goddess.

Forgive me. I'm slightly drunk, and I'm not a classicist anyway.

As it is, then: A monkey doesn't know why he has a wire in his brain, and it would be no easier for him if he did. When I see Thad going through lover after lover and hating them all, Jack getting stoned and losing his job, Ronnie forgetting his name, and Bill staring at his wrists, I can see no point in telling them why Diana left us.

If I did, and they could understand, they'd only realize that our loss had nothing to do with how little she really loved us, or even how little we love each other. It had to do with how much we love ourselves.

Shelby has just come in. I hope she got the job, because she needs another focus, another life jacket, just as I do now that I've finished the paper. For me, the fall semester will begin in three days, bringing the summer to an end. For her, something else will have to serve.

I've moved in with her, and we've bought thick drapes for the bedroom windows. In the night, neither of us can know if the other's eyes are open or closed.

CAPTAIN COYOTE'S LAST HUNT

On the night before a hunt, I would lie awake and listen to them. Even in the oven-hot bedroom, I shivered. Their quavering howls and yips echoed so that it became impossible to guess whether there were two or two hundred of them. They had come close to our houses to dare us.

And so, in the morning, we went after them.

Sometimes when the greyhounds had almost overtaken a coyote, it stopped running. Just stopped, like that. The lead dog, usually Widower, whizzed past and crashed, his legs windmilling, throwing grass and dirt. The other dogs became a tangle. During that moment of chaos, the coyote took off again.

One time, though, it didn't take off, but stood there with its tongue hanging out, laughing at the sight of Widower flailing to a halt. "Don't *you* look stupid!"

But Widower never looked stupid for long, because when he and the other dogs caught a coyote, they ripped it to pieces. Most times they stayed on it until it died, but once in a while they lost interest when it quit struggling. Then the Captain got out of the truck. If the animal was still conscious, he put a few rounds into its belly before the head shot. Sometimes he let me do it.

A hunt on open prairie always ended with a coyote mangled and dead.

Always, except once.

I became the apprentice of Captain Coyote after he dropped out of El Dorado High. This was several months before his

mother kicked him off her property, so he had neither a job nor a reason to get one. Nor, at sixteen, did he have a chance of being drafted yet. What he did have was a .22-caliber pistol, a '61 Chevy pickup, and eleven greyhounds.

I was fourteen. My dad worked as an oil rigger, but not often. My mom would have gotten a job to fill the gaps, but she was already overworked at home. I had two brothers, both younger, both brats. We lived seven miles northeast of El Dorado, Kansas, in a house that was sixty years old and falling apart. Living there in the summer meant eating dust.

My dad had always been strict, but he really started getting after me that summer. He was home most of the time, and if I was home too, I was in trouble. Sometimes he'd knock me around.

So I spent a lot of time with Captain Coyote.

The Captain lived three miles north of us, on the edge of the treeless Flint Hills. Thousands of rolling acres spread out to the north, east, and west, broken only by flash-flood gullies and infrequent barbed wire. That summer, those acres were brown.

The Captain's mother and five of his cousins lived in a house that was even more of a shack than my family's was. When I went to the place, though, my first thought was never that the house was junk. My first thought was *dogshit*. If I stayed more than twenty minutes, my hair and clothes would smell like the stuff all day.

The Captain himself lived in a fourteen-foot aluminum trailer behind his mother's house. Beyond that were the dog pens. Ten of the greyhounds stayed in the biggest pen, and the meanest male, Widower, stayed in a smaller one. The third and smallest pen was reserved for any bitch ready to whelp, but the Captain hadn't needed to use it since spring. The dirt in each pen was packed hard as a sidewalk. Even when the dogs were quiet, the hum of flies was constant.

I arrived for our twelfth hunt on a Friday morning in August. The previous hunt hadn't turned up any coyotes, so the Captain had decided that today we would go farther into the hills than ever before. If we were challenged by a rancher, we would pretend that we each thought the other had taken care of getting permission.

The Captain appeared in the doorway of his trailer as I steered my bike around the chuckholes beside his mother's house. He stood under his baling-wire string of coyote ears and eyed me. "You're late, punk," he said, tugging his shirt over his gut. "Thought you said you'd make it before sunup." The morning was already so bright and hot that the dogshit stank like it was cooking.

I hopped off the bike and let it fall. "Sorry, Captain. My old man's on the warpath. Had to wait until he got pissed at somebody else before I could cut out."

The Captain grunted. "You ever want to borrow my gun to kill that sonofabitch, you let me know." He squinted up at the sun. "I damn near took off without you." But his eyes were crusty, and his straw-like hair was smashed flat on the right side and sticking up on the left. He was wearing greasy jeans, a gray muscle shirt, and dirt-brown boots, but that didn't mean anything because he slept in his clothes.

"Glad you waited," I said.

He grunted again and started for his pickup, which was parked beside the dog pens. I followed. When the greyhounds saw us coming, they went nuts. They were always eager to cram into the boxes, because it meant they would get to kill something. The Captain unbolted the chicken-wire door that covered the four boxes on the left side of the truck bed, and I unbolted the one on the right. The doors were hinged on the bottom, so when they fell open, they made the pickup look as if it had stubby wings growing out of the bed walls.

The Captain got his rubber billy club from the cab and went to the pen where Widower waited. Widower stood almost waist-high to the Captain, and his shoulder and haunch muscles were like boulders under a coat the color of a storm cloud. His name had once been Ralph, but the Captain had changed it after Ralph killed the first bitch he mated with.

170

Widower rose on his hind legs and clamped his jaws onto the club when the Captain put it over the gate. Then the Captain brought him to the truck, where the dog let go of the club and leaped up into the first box on the left, smacking his head on the back wall. He turned to face outward and hunkered down, drooling. The Captain told me to load up seven more, my choice, while he stayed ready to use the club if Widower decided to attack any of them.

I grabbed the three choke chains from the cab and went to the big pen. The first dog to put his front paws on the gate was my favorite, a brindle male named Hacksaw. I let him out so he could run to the truck on his own, and then I chained the next three. They almost yanked my arms out of their sockets as they pulled me to the pickup. Hacksaw was waiting beside the right rear tire, so I helped him up first. When I'd boosted the others as well, I took off their chains and bolted the door. The four dogs grinned out at me, their eyes bright, their tongues dripping.

"Get a move on, punk," Captain Coyote called from the other side. "Widower wants meat."

I ran back to the pen, chained up three more, and then had to chase down a fourth that slipped out. Two of the Captain's snot-nosed cousins appeared as the dog escaped, and they did all they could to get in my way. It took me ten minutes to get the stray back into the pen and bring the others to the left side of the truck.

"Pretty dumbass thing to do," the Captain said. I got the dogs loaded as fast as I could while he smacked Widower to keep him from lunging out at them. The two cousins stood back by the trailer and made faces at me.

When the left door was bolted, the Captain told me to attach the release cables while he went into his mother's house. He returned with a loaf of bread, a package of bologna, and a twelve-pack. The cousins became big-eyed, and they ran into the house. The Captain and I got inside the pickup and headed out. As the truck bounced down the driveway, I looked back and saw the Captain's mother, dressed in a pink ribbed robe, standing on her porch. She was yelling. The Captain had taken her food and beer without asking. A couple of the dogs barked at her, and then we were on the road, leaving billows of brown dirt behind us.

At midday, among scorched hills far north of home, Captain Coyote let the truck crawl beside a gully that lay to our left. He was drinking a beer, but his eyes were intent on the brush at the bottom of the gully. His little revolver waited on the seat between us. I was eating a sandwich and trying to watch the gully as intently as he was. Behind us, the dogs were whining. I thought they must be thirsty, but I knew better than to say so.

"There," the Captain said, dropping his beer and taking up the pistol. As he stopped the pickup, the dogs shifted, rocking us. A few of them yipped.

I peered past the Captain. On the far wall of the gully was a clump of brush with an extra shadow that might have been a den. I never would have spotted it on my own.

The Captain aimed his pistol and fired two shots while he honked the truck horn and yelled. I yelled too, and the dogs went berserk. Two puffs of dust flew from the brush, and then, as if coalescing from that dust, two yellow-brown streaks shot out. They bounded up the wall and dashed into the prairie.

"God damn, *two*!" the Captain yelled. He dropped his gun and yanked on the cable looped around his outside mirror. The left bolt came free with a ping, the chicken- wire door fell, and four greyhounds leaped into the gully. Two of them tumbled as they hit the bottom, but they were up in an instant and racing after the others. Widower, in the lead, was thirty yards into the grass before the fourth dog was out of the gully.

I knotted a fist around the cable on my right. "Want me to cut the others loose? Since there's two?"

The Captain popped the clutch. "Don't touch it until I say!" He drove a few hundred yards to a shallow part of the gully, and we bounced across, almost high-centering on the far side. The dogs in back yelped.

Once past the gully, the Captain drove over the prairie at bone-rattling speed. My beer foamed into my lap. The truck was vibrating so much that I couldn't even see the running greyhounds until we almost hit the dog bringing up the rear. The coyotes were still ahead of the chase, but Widower was closing the gap with every stride.

"Chomp their asses, Widower!" the Captain cried.

The second coyote was trailing the first by a dozen yards, and Widower caught it as the Captain yelled. Widower's favorite takedown was to come up alongside and lock his jaws on a coyote's neck, but this one kept zig-zagging, so he clamped onto its tail instead. The coyote pulled away, leaving him with a mouthful of fur and skin, but he had slowed it enough for the other dogs to catch up. The coyote kicked and snapped, but they piled on and forced it down.

When the Captain stopped beside them, the air already smelled of sour fur and blood. The dogs in the truck were wild with frustration. I looked back and saw them biting the chicken wire. Hacksaw, especially, was hurting himself, and I wished I could let him out. On the ground, one dog was tearing at the coyote's throat, and two were ripping into its side and belly. It was screaming the way that only a coyote can scream.

Widower stood apart. He still had a mouthful of fur, but he seemed unaware of it. He was staring northward, his muscles rigid, his ears pricked.

The first coyote stood atop a hill an eighth of a mile away. It watched as its companion was killed.

"They're okay," the Captain said, nodding at the bloody-muzzled dogs on the ground. "Let's get the other sonofabitch."

When the pickup started moving again, Widower sprinted ahead. He didn't care about the coyote that was already dying. He wanted the one that was still free, and he wanted it before the Captain had me release the rest of the dogs.

The coyote on the hill remained motionless, waiting, as we came within a hundred yards.

"Why don't he run?" I asked.

The Captain didn't answer, but slewed the truck sideways and yelled for me to yank the cable. I did, and the second wave burst out. Hacksaw led the charge.

The coyote waited until Widower was within twenty yards, and then it disappeared over the crest of the hill.

"Bastard's quick," the Captain said as the pursuing greyhounds went after it. He reached for the gearshift, then looked back. The downed coyote wasn't moving at all now, but the dogs who had tackled it were still ripping into it. They would be busy for a while yet.

On the far side of the hill we found a wide bowl webbed with gullies. Widower, Hacksaw, and the coyote were already out of sight in the maze, and the other dogs vanished as we spotted them. The Captain slammed his fist on the dash. Letting the greyhounds run in and out of gully after gully was a good way to get them hurt, and the coyote would probably escape anyway. We drove down to the edge of the nearest gully and got out to call the dogs even though we knew they wouldn't come until they had either killed their prey or given up hope of finding it.

The greyhounds popped up here and there and were making plenty of noise, so the Captain left me to keep track of them while he drove back to collect the other three. That was fine with me, because I'd been sweating in the truck, and it felt good to stand out in the hot breeze and listen to the grass whisper. Besides, my least favorite part of a hunt was getting the dogs off the coyote at the end.

The Captain had been gone less than a minute when one of the dogs in the maze shrieked. It was one long, piercing cry — and then silence. No more yips, no more barks. Nor could I hear the truck on the other side of the hill. I yelled for the Captain, but there was no answer. My voice had been swallowed by the prairie.

174

I jumped into the gully, climbed out the other side, and ran toward the spot where I thought the shriek had come from. I imagined a trap closing on a dog's ankle, a hole breaking his leg, a rattler sinking its fangs into his face. I plunged into another gully and ran down its length, crashing through brush and stumbling over rocks. The walls were as high as my shoulders, and when I looked back toward the hill to see if the Captain was coming, I saw land and sky through rushing brown stems. It was as if the world were lit by a sun-colored strobe. The Captain wasn't coming. I was alone when I found Hacksaw.

He was lying on his side on a bare patch of ground. There was no trap, no hole, no snake. His belly was open.

He was still a little bit alive, and he looked at me as if I should do something. I squatted and put my hand on his head, and he died. I looked away then and saw his three companions from the right side of the truck. They stood a short distance down the gully, staring at us and shifting as if they were caged. One of them whined.

We stayed that way until the Captain arrived. I don't know how he found us. He stood above on the lip of the gully, his pistol in his hand and his club in his belt, his broad face speckled with sweat. "God damn," he said. "Is he dead?"

I nodded, turning so he wouldn't see my eyes. I rubbed my hands on my jeans.

The Captain jumped into the gully, his boots setting off a tumble of rocks and dirt. "What happened?"

"Don't know." I thought my voice sounded almost okay. "I heard him squeal, and I ran over, and I found him like this."

The Captain nudged the body with a boot, and it moved like it was put together with string. He cocked his pistol, squatted, and put the muzzle behind Hacksaw's ear. I watched while he pulled the trigger. The gun went *snap*. Hacksaw's head didn't even twitch.

The other three dogs approached, sniffing, and the Captain took his club from his belt. He yelled "Truck!" and two of them obeyed, jumping out of the gully and trotting to the pickup. The third came all the way to Hacksaw's body and growled. I went to put the first two into their boxes and to fetch a choke chain.

I returned to find the Captain beating the third dog. He was telling her that she was worthless and that she ought to be shot and fed to the others. I moved to where he could see me, and he stopped. "Don't just stand there, punk," he said. "Get her into the God damn truck."

I put the chain on the cringing dog and began tugging her up the wall.

"Where the hell's Widower?" the Captain asked.

"Still after the coyote, I guess," I said. "He don't give up."

The Captain's expression softened. "No, he don't."

I hated Widower. I had never heard of a lone coyote doing anything like what had been done to Hacksaw, but I knew that Widower had already killed at least one other dog. I figured that when Hacksaw got close to the coyote, Widower got pissed off. Or maybe the coyote had already gotten away when Hacksaw showed up, and Widower took out his frustration on him.

I hoped that when Widower returned, there would be evidence of what he had done, and the Captain would use the pistol on him.

It was a stupid hope. The Captain would never shoot Widower, not even to put him out of misery.

When the clubbed bitch was in her box, the Captain came up and began honking the truck horn. After a while, Widower appeared atop a ridge across the bowl and trotted down toward us. The Captain met him as he came out of the gully where Hacksaw lay. Widower clamped onto the billy, and they came to the pickup. There were dark smears at the corners of the greyhound's mouth, and a tuft of brindle fur.

"Look at that," the Captain said. "Traipsed over half the Flint Hills, and he still has some of that coyote's tail in his mouth."

"Uh huh," I said.

Widower jumped into his box, and the Captain bolted the door. Then he looked at me, narrow-eyed. "We'll come back tomorrow and kill the sonofabitch that done that to Hacksaw."

He got into the truck and started the engine.

I looked at the gully. "Ain't we going to — "

"It'll be back for the meat," the Captain said. "That's how we'll nail it."

I got in and saw that he had cut off the dead coyote's ears to add to his string. He drove us back over the hill.

At supper that evening, my dad slapped me in the mouth. I don't remember why. My brothers were acting rotten, but they didn't get smacked. I did.

In the night, I heard the coyotes.

Before sunrise, I got up and dressed quietly so that I wouldn't wake my brothers. One of them woke up anyway, but he watched me without saying anything.

When I was dressed, I went into the kitchen and snuck bread and cheese from the refrigerator. I also took some quarters and dimes from my mom's purse. Then I left the house and rode my bike to Captain Coyote's, carrying the bread and cheese in my left hand while I steered with my right. Halfway there, two deer loped across the road in front of me and jumped a fence. In the predawn gray, they were like floating shadows.

The Captain was loading the dogs when I arrived. He was pleased that I'd brought food, and he said we could buy pop with the money. When we drove away, the two dogs we left behind looked after us with longing. Widower was in his usual box behind the driver's side of the cab.

By the time we reached the hilltop overlooking the maze, the sun had burnt the sky to the color of pale slate. My strawberry soda was warm, so I took one of the Captain's beers from the styrofoam cooler at my feet. I drank half of it in one long pull as we descended into the bowl.

The Captain kept his right hand on his pistol as he maneuvered the truck between the gullies to the place where Hacksaw had been killed. There he stopped and got out, taking the gun. He motioned for me to follow, and we walked to the edge of the

177

gully and looked down.

Hacksaw's body had been stripped of fur and flesh, and his bones were scattered over the gully floor. Flies had gathered on his head.

"God damn," the Captain said.

I couldn't blame Widower for this.

The Captain went into the gully. He kicked a few of the bones and then squatted to examine the ground. "The sonofabitches dragged off the whole back half," he said. "Ain't many tracks, but there had to be at least four or five of 'em." He stood and climbed back up the wall. "They ain't so smart, though. I can see the drag marks."

We got back into the truck, and the Captain drove slowly, following marks that I couldn't make out. As we wound our way farther into the maze, the day became hotter, and the dogs whined. I finished my beer and then sucked on ice from the cooler. The Captain wiped his forehead with the back of his gun hand. Near the center of the bowl, I saw that while he watched the gully on our left, another was angling toward us on the right. We were driving on a wedge of prairie that was becoming smaller and smaller.

"We're running out of land," I said.

"Shut up. I know it."

We reached the end, and the Captain stopped the pickup. The front tires were on the edges, and dirt crumbled into both gullies. The dogs rocked us.

The Captain killed the engine and opened his door, telling me to stay put. Outside, he checked to be sure that all six chambers of his pistol were loaded. "If I yell, or if you hear more than one shot," he said, "cut Widower's bunch loose."

"Even if they can't see the coyote?"

"They'll hear the shots. If I keep on yelling, cut the others loose too." He pulled his billy from under the seat and stuck it in his belt, then closed the door and tightened the release cable. "When the second bunch is out, you can come along." He jumped down into the big gully where the two smaller ones joined.

I watched him walk away. He held his pistol ready at his side. When he was about thirty yards distant, he went around a curve. The gully was so deep that I couldn't even see his head now.

I took another beer from the cooler, scooted to the driver's side, and waited. Behind me, the greyhounds scratched and whined. They were ready. I was afraid that the coyotes that had eaten Hacksaw would be torn up or shot before I could be there.

Between the sun and the beer, I dozed off. Widower's growl brought me awake. When I opened my eyes, I saw the coyote.

It stood in the grass on the far side of the gully, watching me with yellow eyes. It was scrawny, and its fur was mottled and mangy, but it held itself as if it were perfect. It wasn't all that interested in me. Just looking. Having nothing better to do at the moment.

At its feet lay part of a brindle haunch.

I sat stock-still. The dogs were barking and clawing at the chicken wire. I didn't know what to do. The Captain had ordered me to wait for his signal. I thought of honking the horn to alert him, but that might scare off the coyote. Anything I did would be wrong.

Slowly, as if the air were syrup, I took my left hand from the armrest. My eyes stayed locked with the ones across the gully. As my fingers closed on the cable, the coyote yawned.

The bolt came free, and the dogs hit the door. Three of them landed on the ground beside the truck before plunging into the gully, but Widower leaped all the way to the gully's center. Another leap took him halfway up the far wall. The coyote was still watching me as Widower exploded into the grass.

But when the greyhound lunged, the coyote was suddenly two feet to the right of where it had been. Widower shot past, his jaws closing on air.

The coyote was still looking right at me. But now, instead of mild interest, I saw something else in its eyes.

179

Don't you *look stupid!*

I punched the horn.

The coyote wheeled and ran, becoming a blur. Widower changed direction and raced after it. The other three dogs came out of the gully and paused, sniffing at the part of Hacksaw that the coyote had left. Then one of them took off, and the rest followed.

The chase went into and out of gullies, heading in the direction that the Captain had taken. When the coyote came in view of the dogs on the right side of the truck, I leaned across and yanked that cable too. Then I blew three more blasts on the horn and shoved my door open.

I fell going down the wall, but scrambled up at the bottom and ran, shouting a warning to the Captain. I couldn't see any of the the greyhounds now, but I heard sporadic barking. I was sure that they were all in the same gully as me, running somewhere ahead in its twisting path.

The barking stopped and was replaced by wild snarls. The dogs had caught the coyote.

Then came a shriek like the one I'd heard the day before. Then another. Then a shouted curse and two snaps like fire-crackers. The Captain was calling for help. There were more shrieks. I tried to run faster. The gully widened before me.

When I found them, five of the dogs were dead. The coyote stood in a circle of torn bodies, its muzzle shining with blood. The Captain and his three remaining dogs were backed against a wall. The two smaller ones were cringing, but Widower still snarled. He strained to attack, but the Captain held him by the back of the neck. The Captain's free hand gripped his pistol. It was pointing at the coyote.

The coyote regarded them with the same look of semi-bore-dom with which it had regarded me. It wasn't snarling. All it did was twitch its tail a little. It showed no interest in the bodies of the five greyhounds.

I had stopped several yards away, and it was only when I

took a step backward that the Captain saw me. "Throw me a choke chain!" he yelled. "If Widower gets loose, that thing'll kill him! It's got rabies!"

I looked back at the coyote. It wasn't rabid. It grinned at the Captain, letting its tongue loll.

My chest tightened. "What are you?" I whispered.

The Captain glared at me. "A chain, God damn it! Throw me a chain, punk!"

But I didn't have one. I had run from the truck in a blind frenzy, and I hadn't thought of anything. I tasted sweat. "I'll have to go back," I babbled. "I'll hurry, Captain, I'll —"

His look froze me. "It's too late," he said. Then he squinted at the coyote, and his pistol arm stiffened.

Widower broke free, and the Captain fired. A red streak ripped down the coyote's shoulder. It didn't flinch. But as the greyhound reached it, it dodged, and Widower hit the opposite wall. He spun and charged again.

His rage had infected the other two dogs, and they charged as well. For a moment, I thought they had a chance because the coyote was facing Widower, but as they jumped, it whirled. When they hit the ground, they were screaming. Their bellies had been torn open.

As the two died, Widower landed hard on the coyote's back and sank his teeth into its neck. His momentum forced it to the dirt, and the Captain roared.

Widower weighed over a hundred pounds, and the coyote couldn't have weighed more than fifty. Yet the coyote stood and began a mad dance, flinging Widower about like a whip. But Widower held on, and below his jaws, the coyote's fur turned dark.

"Break its neck, God damn it!" the Captain yelled. "Break it, break it, break it!"

My eyes and throat burned. I wanted to go stand with the Captain and add my voice to his, but I couldn't. I was afraid.

Abruptly, the coyote stopped. For several seconds, it looked at the Captain while Widower tried to snap its spine. No matter how hard the greyhound strained, the coyote neither moved nor showed any sign of pain.

The Captain started toward them. He had taken only a few steps when the coyote grasped Widower's left foreleg and bit down. I heard the bone crunch before Widower shrieked.

The Captain rushed forward, crying out with his dog, and put the pistol against the coyote's head.

But even as Widower shrieked, he kept his teeth in the coyote's neck, and when the Captain pulled the trigger, the coyote moved. The bullet hit Widower in the right shoulder, and he let go and fell.

The coyote trotted away, hopping over one of the dead greyhounds, and then turned to look at the Captain again.

The Captain was staring down at Widower. The dog lay on his left side, writhing. His shoulder was bleeding.

"Oh please," the Captain said.

At last, I was able to start toward him.

But I was too slow. He looked up from Widower, faced the coyote, and began walking. The coyote waited for him. I began to run.

The Captain stood before the coyote and pointed his pistol, and the coyote rose on its hind legs and snapped at his hand. The Captain jerked, and the gun flew from his grasp. It landed at the base of the gully wall, and I turned toward it.

The Captain yanked his club from his belt and lunged. But the coyote dodged again, and the Captain lost his balance. His club tumbled away. As he hit the ground, the coyote took his ankle in its mouth.

My hands closed on the gun, but as I fumbled to aim, Widower stood, holding his crushed leg in the air. He leaped onto the coyote for the second time, and they rolled away from the Captain.

The Captain looked up. His cheek was scraped.

Widower couldn't stay on top. The coyote got out from under him in an eyeblink, and then it started nipping. It nipped at his neck, his ribs, his legs, his tail. It opened a dozen wounds, moving too fast for the crippled greyhound to defend himself, and giving me no clear shot.

The coyote stripped the fur and skin from Widower's tail, and then from his right foreleg. Widower collapsed again, his snarl melting into a cry like a puppy's.

I was about to shoot when the Captain crawled between me and my target. "That's enough, you sonofabitch," he said to the coyote.

The coyote eyed him for a moment, then lowered its head and bit off Widower's left ear. Widower yelped.

"God," the Captain said. "God damn."

The coyote dropped the severed ear and tore off the other one. This time, Widower only whimpered.

The coyote took both ears in its mouth and began trotting off down the gully.

The Captain got to his feet and lurched forward. I was afraid that he would attack the coyote again, but he only went as far as Widower. He knelt beside the dog and stroked his head, murmuring words I couldn't hear.

The coyote continued on, without looking back.

I had never hated anything so much.

Suddenly I was past the Captain, past Widower, past the seven dead greyhounds, and coming up behind it. It turned to wait for me. I slowed to a walk and held the pistol before me with both hands. There were two rounds left. One for each yellow eye.

When I stopped, the coyote and I were separated by less than four feet. It looked at me with the same expression as before. It was bleeding, and flies were already buzzing around the wound on its shoulder. It was only a coyote.

I squeezed the trigger. There was a loud snap, and dust flew up on the coyote's right. I squeezed again, and dust flew up on its left. It hadn't moved.

I pulled the trigger again and again, as if something more than a click would happen by magic. When I finally quit, the coyote grinned at me around Widower's ears.

Don't you *look stupid!*

And then I knew it. It was the thing that hardly noticed us, and hardly cared when it did. It was the thing that came close in the night and taunted, knowing we could never catch it.

It was why my dad was what he was. It was why Captain Coyote set his dogs on things that were free.

It was what the Captain called on when he swore.

The coyote's grin faded. It regarded me for a few more moments before turning and trotting away again. I watched until it was gone, and then I lowered the pistol. I spotted the billy club on the ground and retrieved it. My arms and legs were numb.

The Captain was still cradling Widower's head when I went to him. He didn't respond to my voice, but he looked up when I held out his pistol and club. He accepted them, and then he stood. Together, we carried Widower to the truck. The dog had stopped whimpering, but he was still breathing. We left the others behind.

I didn't get home until after midnight. Luckily, my dad was out somewhere. My mom just gave me one of her sad looks and told me that I had almost worried her to death.

I lay awake for a long time, listening to the sounds of my brothers sleeping. A few hours before dawn, those sounds mingled with distant yips and howls that echoed forever. There might have been two of them, or two hundred.

Maybe there were as many as they wanted.

Thanks to the Captain and the antibiotics he stole, Widower lived. I visited them often during the convalescence, but it was a hard thing to do, because the dog looked like hell. The ear ridges were ragged and ugly. The last wound to heal was the stripped right foreleg, which stayed pink and raw long after the left foreleg was fine again. In the evenings, it gleamed in the weak light inside the trailer. Widower was an indoor dog now.

He became fat and dull-eyed.

On each of my visits, the Captain told me how lucky he was to have a dog like this. "Those coyotes would have torn out my God damn throat," he said, "but Widower took on the whole pack." After the greyhound was healthy again, the Captain was going to breed him. Then, when there were enough dogs, they would go back into the hills and have their revenge. I was invited.

The Captain had not seen what I had.

After school started, my trips to the Captain's became less frequent. By Thanksgiving, I wasn't going at all. At Christmas, I heard that his mother had run him off, and that he had moved his trailer to Hutchinson. Later, someone said he'd gone into the service. No one mentioned his dogs.

I didn't see him again until last month. I was walking through the plant on my way to a meeting, and there he was, punching rivets. I almost went past, but then he saw me too, and I had to stop.

I shook his hand and called him Captain. His face locked up as if I'd knifed him, and I knew that sometime, somewhere, he had met it again. And had seen.

I would have left then, but I'd been to college, and I knew how to be polite. So I asked him the safe questions you ask when you haven't seen someone in twenty years, the questions that can be answered with generalities or lies. He'd been in the Marines. Then he'd worked in a machine shop in Texas. Then he'd moved back to home ground, to Wichita. He'd hired on at the plant just two days before.

I didn't ask about Widower.

He didn't ask about me.

I started to tell him that my father was dead, then decided not to. I shook his hand again and went to my meeting.

I try not to go through that part of the plant anymore, but sometimes I have to. On those occasions, I wave and say hello, and he nods.

When I say hello, I call him Duane.

THE CHAFF HE WILL BURN

Amanda's parents hated each other, and they didn't seem to like her either. They expected her to be perfect, and she wasn't. So one Sunday night in June, while most of Spring Hill slept, seven-year-old Amanda lay awake and decided to burn herself to death in public.

Earlier that day, in Sunday School, she had learned that martyrs for Jesus were mourned more thoroughly than just about anyone. She had therefore resolved to become a martyr as soon as possible, and had asked her teacher to explain the requirements.

Her teacher said that the first martyr, Stephen, had set a precedent by provoking a mob of Jews into stoning him. Despite that precedent, however, other methods of martyrdom had become accepted over the years.

Some martyrs were stabbed with swords.

Some were crushed under boulders.

Some were pierced through and through with arrows.

Some were fed to lions.

Some were tortured with hot irons and then dragged by the ankles to dungeons, their heads bumping on stone steps as they descended.

Some were crucified upside-down.

Some were stretched on racks or between oxen until they came apart.

Some were burned at the stake.

Some were placed in towers where the wind whistled

through slits and tormented them until they clawed their ears to shreds and died of madness.

There was a lot to choose from.

Amanda got out of bed and went to a corner of her room to stand on her head. She wasn't able to stay there for long, though, because she had a runny nose and could feel the mucus pooling up behind her eyes. Upside-down crucifixion, she decided, wouldn't do.

Once in bed again, she imagined herself being stoned. The scenario was appealing (how her parents would cringe as each rock struck her face!), but she had to reject it because she didn't think she could find a mob of Jews in central Nebraska.

It occurred to her then that most of the other methods of martyrdom had a similar drawback. They required the assistance of non-Christians, and she didn't know any.

The only method that she felt she could handle by herself was that of burning. Ideally, it was supposed to be "burning at the stake," which implied both a stake and someone to tie her to it. But surely a stake was secondary; the fire was the thing.

The more she thought about it, the more she liked the idea. A fire was something people couldn't help noticing — and if she had a sizable audience, they would talk about the event for years to come. Future generations of Spring Hill children would grow up hearing the story.

Such an audience, she realized, was only a few days away. Spring Hill's annual fair, the Summer Celebration, was to be held at the park the very next weekend, and her Sunday School class was scheduled to sing on Friday evening. It would be perfect.

Amanda hardly slept that night. (She might not have been able to sleep anyway, because her parents were yelling.) She didn't know how she would be able to contain her excitement through the coming week.

On Friday evening, Amanda's sno-cone melted to green water that stained her hands. Flies kept landing on her fingers

187

to eat the sugar.

She crushed the paper cone and threw it into a barrel. Then she asked her mother if she could go to the car to wash her hands with the water jug. Her nose was still runny, and she sniffled as she spoke.

Amanda's mother gave her the car keys and told her to go directly to the amphitheater as soon as her hands were clean. She wasn't even looking at Amanda, but at Amanda's father, who was talking to a high-school girl at the Pop the Balloons booth.

The sun had gone behind the steeple of the Methodist church when Amanda unlocked the car and climbed into the front seat. The clock on the dash showed that twelve minutes remained until her class had to sing. She took a book of matches from the ashtray and watched the clock count off seconds with blinking dots.

After five minutes, she looked out to see whether her parents were coming to check on her. Neither of them was. The strings of lights on the carnival rides had been turned on, though, and they were pretty. Amanda rolled down the window to hear the grunts and roars of the engines and the happy cries of the people being whirled around.

When it was time, she went outside and opened the car trunk. The red two-gallon gasoline can that her father kept for emergencies was wedged between the spare tire and the left wheel well. It was stuck tight, but came free after four hard tugs. The gasoline inside sloshed, and the walls of the can went *boing-boom, boing-boom*. Amanda set the can on the pavement and twisted off the cap with her sticky hands. The gasoline had a sharp, delicious stink.

Amanda threw the cap into the trunk, picked up the can, and went back into the park. The can was heavy, so she carried it with both hands, crushing the matchbook against the handle. She had to walk bowlegged, and gasoline splashed onto her wrists. It made the fine hair on her arms stand up. Some of the people she passed looked at her, but no one spoke to her.

As she approached the amphitheater, the noise of the rides was replaced by the sound of applause. The five- and six-year-olds' Sunday School class had finished singing, and Amanda's class would be taking the stage at any moment.

She hurried through a cluster of evergreens to the edge of the amphitheater, and then she paused to look out at her audience. Forty or fifty parents, plus several old folks from the nursing home, were sitting on lawn chairs and blankets. At the bottom of the slope stood a wooden platform illuminated by portable floodlights. The five- and six-year-olds were trooping down steps at one end, and Amanda's classmates were ascending steps at the other.

She took a breath and burst from the evergreens, running through the audience with the can banging against her knees. When she reached the platform, she stumbled up the steps where the last of the younger children was coming off. Then, as she sat cross-legged in the center of the stage, she glimpsed her parents. They were rising from the ground like open-mouthed ghosts.

Amanda dropped the matches, lifted the gasoline can over her head, and turned it upside-down. The fuel came out in gouts, and the can lurched. Amanda gasped as the first splash drenched her hair and face, but she only closed her eyes for a second. The gasoline was cold, and the fumes choked her, but she held on until her dress was soaked.

By the time she dropped the can, the people in the audience were yelling. Some were coming toward her. Amanda glanced to one side and saw her classmates standing on the steps. They looked like plastic dolls.

As she faced the audience again, she saw her parents struggling through a jumble of people and lawn chairs. She tore a match from the book and touched its head to the black strip on the cover.

The match caught with a sputter that Amanda heard over the shouting, and the flame blossomed like a yellow flower. It touched a fold of her dress, and the world became a blaze of gold.

189

There were shadows beyond the wall of that world, moving like fish seen from the surface of a lake on a sunny day. She wondered what they were.

When Amanda's parents began planning their separation that winter, they stopped taking her to the psychologist in Grand Island. They needed their money for lawyers.

Amanda hadn't liked the psychologist, but he had been better than the medical doctors. They had poked and probed and drawn blood, and then all they had said was that it must have been sweat. Sweat, they said, was what protected the feet of firewalkers.

None of them really knew why she had failed. Neither did she, even though her classmates told her everything that had happened after she lit the match:

A man from the audience burned his hands slapping at the fire. Someone else tried to smother it with a blanket, but the blanket ignited. People ran around and screamed.

Finally, Amanda's father threw a quilt that he had plunged into the tank at the dunking booth, and Amanda fell over as it covered her. Even then, she and the surrounding boards burned for a while.

Afraid to look at what Amanda might have become, her parents put another blanket over the ruined quilt and wrapped their daughter like a mummy. They took the bundle to the county hospital.

Amanda remembered what had happened next:

When a doctor and a nurse cut away the blanket and rags, she gazed up at them. They stared back.

Her clothes and shoes were gone. So was her hair, including the wisps on her arms and legs. Her skin was smooth and pink.

She didn't even feel the sting that she would have felt from a sunburn. Her runny nose was cured.

Later, while leaving the hospital, she saw a man with white bandages on his hands. He was the one who had tried to slap down her flames. He hadn't even come within four feet of her before being driven back.

Amanda could only conclude that Jesus disliked her. She had tried to become a martyr, but trying had not been good enough. She would have to find out what was.

Amanda's mother left Spring Hill on the day after New Year's, taking Amanda with her. Amanda's father wasn't home at the time. Outside, it was snowing, and Amanda helped brush off the car before getting in.

They moved to Sheldon, a town on the other side of Grand Island. Amanda's hair was almost as long now as it had been before the Summer Celebration, so no one at her new school or church would know that she had set herself on fire. That was fine with her. She didn't want to be reminded of her failure.

Amanda came to like life in Sheldon. For one thing, there was no more yelling. Her mother went to work at a bank every day while she was at school, and in the evenings they ate supper from TV trays and watched reruns of *M*A*S*H*. One weekend a month, Amanda stayed with her father in Spring Hill, and he taught her the rules of football. One Saturday in October, he took her all the way to Lincoln, and they saw the Cornhuskers beat Kansas 57 to 3. After the sixth touchdown, Amanda wrapped her arms around her father's neck and cheered.

Seven years passed, and Amanda almost forgot about wanting to be a martyr. Then, in the summer that she turned fourteen, her father took his girlfriend to the Virgin Islands. Before leaving, he gave Amanda a leatherbound Bible with a concordance for a birthday present. She put it away in a drawer without opening it. The little Gideon New Testament she had been given at Sunday School in Spring Hill was good enough for her.

While her father was on St. Croix, her mother talked to her about sex. Amanda protested that she'd had a sex education class in eighth grade, but her mother replied that what they were going to discuss wasn't covered in textbooks. The books might

191

make it all seem quite clean, she said, but it wasn't. It was dirty and awful, and boys would use it to hurt Amanda if she let them. She was pretty, and boys liked to hurt things that were pretty. This was because Cain had killed Abel. Abel had been gentle, but when he died, it meant that all men would be descended from brutality.

Amanda would have to be good, or she would regret it.

Amanda promised that she would be better than good.

In Sheldon, being in ninth grade meant that Amanda went to high school. The biggest change was that her friends, all of whom were girls, wanted her to do more things after school hours. She would sometimes join them for movies or slee-povers, but she refused to attend school parties, dances, or even football games. There would be boys there.

She had no problems until May. Then, while she was walking home one afternoon, an older boy caught up with her and asked her to the prom. Amanda stammered that she didn't think she could go, but the boy suggested that she ask her mother. She turned down the wrong street to get away from him.

All that evening, she tried to think of a way to tell her mother what had happened, but at eleven o'clock she went to bed without having said a word about it.

In the morning, three of Amanda's friends met her at her locker and said that she was the luckiest girl in school. Fresh-men girls were hardly ever asked to the prom, and the boy who had asked her was athletic and popular.

Amanda told them that her mother wouldn't let her go, and that she didn't have a formal dress anyway. Her friends insisted that if her mother was inflexible, there were ways around it. Further-more, a formal was no problem. One of the girls was Amanda's size, and she had a bridesmaid's dress that would be suitable.

For the next six hours, with notes and whispers, Amanda's friends tried to convince her. Again and again, she told them no. But after school, when the boy approached her, she said yes. The rest of the way home, she ached with the lies she would tell.

On Saturday evening, Amanda's date pulled his car away from her friend's driveway and steered with his elbows as he lit a cigarette. Amanda would have to wash her hair at her friend's house before going home in the morning. The boy offered her a cigarette too, but she declined. Her voice sounded like that of a cartoon mouse.

The boy put his cigarettes and butane lighter in the glove compartment, and his hand brushed Amanda's bare arm. She flinched. As he took the car onto the highway and headed for Lincoln, he complimented her dress and her hair. She thanked him, but he seemed to be waiting for something else. Maybe she was supposed to compliment his clothes and hair, too. But that would be stupid, because he was wearing a rented blue tuxedo that was like any other, and his hair looked both stiff and greasy.

When Amanda and her date walked into the hotel ballroom, a huge, pimply boy asked them if they'd brought any Everclear. Amanda's date answered that it was in the back seat of his car, and the pimply boy told him to leave it there for now. The punch here was already spiked, so they would save the extra bottle for the party afterwards. Nobody had told Amanda anything about a party afterwards.

Her date seated her at a table and brought her a plastic goblet of punch. She drank most of it before remembering what was in it. Then two more couples sat at the table and started talking with her date about a horror movie. Amanda hadn't seen it, so she looked at the decorations. Hundreds of silver stars were taped to the walls and suspended on threads from the ceiling. They looked as if they might fall and cut her.

The lights dimmed, a rock band started playing, and Amanda's date asked her to dance. She didn't mind the fast songs, but during the slow ones, the boy pressed too close. When the third slow song started, she asked him to bring her another goblet of punch. This got him away for a while, so she did it twice more. By the time the band stopped, Amanda was dizzy.

Her date took her out of the hotel among a stream of other tuxedos and formal dresses. When they were in the car again, he asked if she wanted to go to the party even though she hadn't brought a change of clothes. He sounded as if he expected her to say yes. She told him that she was sorry, but that she didn't feel well. She hoped he understood and that she hadn't ruined his evening.

The boy smiled. Amanda hadn't ruined anything, he said. Of course he understood.

Amanda thanked him.

He moved closer and said that she didn't have to cry. He reached up and rubbed her cheek with his thumb.

Amanda wasn't crying, but she supposed it was possible, in the weak light, for the boy to mistake her perspiration for tears. She tried not to flinch from his thumb.

Then he was too close, and his mouth was over hers. She put her hands on his shoulders, thinking to push him away, but he only grasped her own shoulders and held her still. She stared at his forehead, where a third eye had appeared over his other two.

The boy's left hand went down inside the front of her dress. Amanda heard laughter and whistles, and she shoved the boy hard. He took his hand away and fell back, bumping his head on his window.

Through the windshield, Amanda saw three boys grinning at her. There were girls, too, hiding their mouths behind their hands.

Amanda unlatched her door. Her date rubbed the back of his head and asked what the big deal was.

She took his butane lighter from the glove compartment and grabbed a bottle wrapped in a paper bag from the back seat. The boy lunged toward her then, but she escaped outside. As she walked to the rear of the car, he got out and yelled at her.

She sat cross-legged on the cement, her hair brushing the car's bumper. She pulled the bag off the half-gallon bottle and twisted the cap, snapping the tax seal.

Her date and several of his friends had gathered around her. Some were laughing, but others looked concerned. They said she was fucked up and should be taken home.

Amanda removed the cap and poured alcohol over her hair and her friend's dress.

Her date stepped forward and reached down to take the bottle away. It was almost empty, so she let him. Then she lit the butane lighter and brought the flame to a ruffle.

Her date and his friends vanished behind blue light.

The dress and stockings melted. Somewhere, somebody shouted about a gas tank, and the blue light was engulfed by a brilliant orange. A flake of ash whispered against Amanda's cheek, and she tried to follow it upward.

On Memorial Day, Amanda and her mother moved back to Spring Hill to live with her father again. Amanda rode with her father in the rental truck, and although he tried to make conversation, he didn't look at her. When they reached his expensive new house-with-a-swimming-pool, his English setter came out to meet them. Amanda stepped from the truck, and the dog ran behind the house.

At dusk, when Amanda tired of putting her things away, she went downstairs for a glass of juice. The smell of charcoal-grilled hamburgers drifted into the kitchen through a sliding screen. Amanda's father and mother were on the pinewood deck by the pool, and her mother was saying that she hoped her father knew she didn't really want to be here. She was only doing it because she couldn't deal with Amanda by herself anymore. She couldn't continue to sleep alone in the same house as a girl who looked like an alien from the cover of the *Weekly World News*. Amanda's father replied that Amanda would look fine when her hair grew back, and that her mother was being a bitch.

That was easy for him to say, Amanda's mother retorted. He hadn't had to live with the child all this time. He had been busy

getting rich and committing adultery.

Amanda's father said it wasn't his fault that a certain person wouldn't give him a divorce.

The argument grew louder and louder, as had all of the arguments that Amanda remembered from when she was little. She left the kitchen without getting any juice, and went into the bathroom to stare at the mirror.

She was bald, with a faint gray shade where her new hair would come in. Her brow ridges were naked and pale, making her eyes look like holes. No wonder the dog had run from her.

She looked like a corpse, but she was alive. Despite her virtue, Jesus had denied her again. It was some consolation, at least, that she had blown up her date's car.

Still not good enough for Heaven, Amanda sat on the toilet lid to wait. Sooner or later, her parents would stop yelling at each other long enough to shout that the hamburgers were ready.

But when the yelling stopped, it was replaced by shrieks and by the dog's frantic yelps. Amanda ran out to the deck and found it ablaze. The charcoal grill had fallen over, and the bottle of lighter fluid had spilled. Amanda's mother was in the pool, screaming, and her father was dancing wildly among the flames. His "Barbecue Genius" apron was burning. On the other side of the pool, his dog was throwing a fit.

Amanda knew what had happened. The argument had become physical, and her father had started shoving. Her mother had shoved back, and one of them had collided with the grill. Amanda considered leaving them like this.

But that might mean that they would become martyrs before she did.

She dashed into the fire and shoved her father hard, like a Cornhusker tackle hitting a Kansas halfback. He stumbled across the deck and fell into the water beside Amanda's mother. His apron was snuffed out. The dog jumped in and swam to him.

As her parents floundered, Amanda sat on the deck so that her clothes would ignite. This time, she watched the process carefully. The fire had not quite consumed all of the fabric when her father came out of the pool with a plastic bucket and doused her. Soon, he had extinguished the fire on the deck as well.

For the third time, the flames had done nothing more than kiss Amanda's skin.

She picked up a soggy hamburger from the blackened deck, and as she ate it, her father bellowed at her to get the hell to her room. She didn't know why he was angry with her, and she told him so. She had saved him, hadn't she? She could have let the whole place burn, couldn't she? After all, it wouldn't have hurt *her*.

But then, having said that, she followed his order. She heard her mother sobbing behind her.

Still wearing her wet, charred rags, Amanda sat on her bed and pondered. She decided that she could understand why Jesus might have objected to her first and second attempts at martyrdom. The first time, she had done it solely for attention, and the second time, she had done it in a place where she should not have been. Such were probably not the ways of true martyrs.

But this third time had been different. She had kept her family from harm, and except for them, she'd had no audience. Nor had she started the fire herself. What was Jesus' objection now?

She no longer had a Sunday School teacher, so there was only one place where she might find an answer. She dug out the leatherbound Bible her father had given her, and then used the concordance to guide her search.

Twenty minutes later, she had her answer at last. It was the only one possible.

She was wheat.

Her parents, and most other people, were chaff.

It wasn't that Jesus disliked her. It was the opposite. Martyrdom was a worthy goal for mortals, but Amanda was beyond that.

Martyrs were mourned. Angels were exalted.

There was a knock at her door, and her parents opened it without waiting for permission. They stared at her rags.

Her father said that he was sorry for having yelled at her. She had done the right thing. He had just been worked up because of the situation, was all.

Amanda told him that she forgave him. For now. He frowned, but said nothing.

Then, in a voice like that of a cartoon mouse, Amanda's mother asked if there was anything she wanted.

Amanda smiled at them.

"You'll be the first to know," she said, and went back to her reading.

A Conflagration Artist

The Amazing Evelyn emerges from the one illuminated door and walks toward the tower at the center of the arena. Her two female assistants, who have been talking with me, fall silent. The other workers who have been milling about fall silent as well. The only sound is the soft crunch of the Amazing Evelyn's slippers on the gritty floor, echoing from the distant, invisible walls.

For her so-called "practice" dive she is wearing a costume similar to the one she will wear tomorrow: a blue swimsuit dotted with silver spangles; white tights; and a silver cape tied at her neck. Her arms are bare. As she approaches I can see the pink ridges and puckers that mar her skin. Or perhaps, in her view, they perfect it. They cause me to look up for a moment at the tower's apex, at the yellow flame burning on the platform there. I am struck again by the incongruity of the television term, *conflagrationary performance art*. Surely this is inappropriate; a "conflagration" is a fire that affects all, wounds all. But here, the Amazing Evelyn will burn alone.

Then I look down from the flame, all the way down, to the surface of the water in the tank beside me. The water is only as deep as my shoulder. I reach over the rim to touch its cool surface with my finger, and the ripples dance across the reflections of the arena lights, splintering them into shards of white.

I look at the Amazing Evelyn again and see that her eyes are focused on me as she comes around the tank. Her hair is amber stubble, a faint shade on her scalp. It is the same color as her eyes. I have seen photographs of her when her hair was long, as have we all. She was one of the most beautiful women in the Midwest then. But today, despite her scars — or because of them? — she is the most beautiful woman in the world.

She stops before me. Her scent is acrid and compelling. I am so surprised that I almost forget to look for a sheen of protective ointment on her skin. I do not forget, though; her beauty and scent are stunning, but I am here as a journalist, and I will do my job. I look her over and see no ointment. Perhaps, then, her costume is impregnated with a flame-retardant chemical. But I do not dare to reach out and touch the fabric. That would be testing a goddess.

Of this, however, I am now certain: Her arms, shoulders, neck, and head are unprotected, as are the tops of her breasts. Her scars bear witness.

"You will not be allowed in the arena tomorrow," she says. These are the first words she has spoken to me. Her voice is like the touch of a feather.

I tell her that I do not understand why she has said this.

"You have been gawking at me all week," she says. "I have allowed it because my management made the agreement, but we are under no obligation to allow you to attend the performance tomorrow."

I point out that anyone with a hundred dollars may attend the performance tomorrow.

"Anyone but you," she says. "I am not a freak to be gawked at."

But the people who will come tomorrow will do so precisely because they do consider her a freak to be gawked at. I do not speak this thought aloud; I do not say anything at all. She knows as well as I do why they are coming. But she needs their money, and so will prostitute herself for them in order to do as she pleases for another year. I am told that she dives at least once a month, sometimes twice a month, for no audience but her assistants and a video camera. But there is no money in that,

201

and she and her assistants must live. So she signed the contract that requires her to dive once a year for a live audience and pay-per-view television. It is clear that she often regrets the arrangement; but she is a woman of honor, and will fulfill her obligations.

She steps around me and walks to the base of the tower. There her assistants attempt to remove her cape, and she stops them.

"We have to give our journalist a good show," she says.

Her voice is bitter, and I am ashamed. She believes I am here to exploit her, and I suppose that I have not given her reason to believe otherwise.

But I know her better than she thinks.

She was married for seven years and gave birth to three children. Her husband's given name was Zachary. The oldest child, a boy, was named Ezekiel; the girl, two years younger, was Emily; the baby, another boy, was Ezra. They lived in a farmhouse in north-central Kansas, where Zachary tended fields of wheat and soybeans.

Their lives seemed neither bleak nor mysterious to their neighbors; nor would they seem so to anyone who could view the Super 8 movies shot by Evelyn. In one of these films, the family has a picnic beside a tree-shaded creek. Zachary eats a chicken leg and winks at the camera; the children's faces become smeared with potato salad. Then the scene shifts to an arched stone bridge that spans the creek, and the children race across it toward the camera. But Ezekiel, who must be six years old, has eaten too much. He holds his distended little belly as he runs, and Emily wins the race. The toddler, Ezra, lags far behind, laughing and flapping his arms. Ezekiel staggers toward the camera, close to tears, and his mouth forms the words, "I lost." Then Zachary comes into view and picks up Ezekiel to comfort him. Emily dances a victory dance, and Ezra spits up on his shirt.

It all appears sweet and normal, and perhaps it was. But Evelyn, serving as camerawoman, appears in none of the films. While the faces of Zachary and the children betray no darkness or despair, hers might have told a different story. We shall never know.

What we do know is that one summer evening during supper, Zachary and Evelyn argued. The argument itself, according to Evelyn's later testimony, was over the fact that Evelyn was serving pork chops too often for Zachary's taste. It seems more likely, however, that the real source of distress was the fact that they were losing the farm. The bank was about to foreclose.

But of human motivations, one can never be sure.

In the midst of the argument, Evelyn ran from the kitchen table and out of the house. (I imagine her wearing an apron over a blue cotton dress, crying as she runs.) She ran across the yard and down the dirt road that passed before their farm. Here there were no trees. The evening was hot and dusty. Evelyn ran almost a mile, and walked a mile farther. Then she started back.

When she drew near the house, she saw black smoke rising from the kitchen windows. She began running again, shouting for Zachary, but Zachary did not answer. Much later, he was found in his soybean field, smeared with dirt, speaking in tongues.

In the kitchen Evelyn discovered the bodies of her children lying on the table, burning. Evelyn beat at the flames with her hands and with a dishrag, and after some minutes, during which her arms blistered and her hair burned, was able to extinguish the fire. But the children were dead, and had been dead before they were set ablaze. Autopsies revealed that Zachary had stabbed each child in the chest before dousing them all with kerosene.

Such events do not bear much commentary. But of the events that followed, more can be said.

After Zachary's trial, conviction, and imprisonment, Evelyn vanished for over a year. No one who knew her, not even her mother or pastor, had any evidence of where she had gone or what she might be doing. Her mother feared that she had disappeared in order to commit suicide. Others, including her pastor, were more inclined to believe that she had left to begin a new life elsewhere under another name, thus wiping out the horror of her children's deaths at the hands of their father.

Then, the following autumn, Evelyn returned. She would not say where she had been or what she had been doing, but moved back into her and Zachary's house as if to resume her former life. By now, though, the bank had taken the fields, and the house would have followed soon had not Evelyn's pastor collected money for her.

It was on the day the pastor delivered the check that Evelyn's new vocation was discovered.

"I was turning into the driveway when I saw her," the pastor told me. "I wouldn't have thought to look up, but the fire caught my eye."

What he saw was Evelyn standing atop the windmill behind the house. As he watched, she dove off, burning, into the water tank at the windmill's base.

"But I couldn't see the tank," the pastor said. "I just saw her disappear behind the house. I thought she was dead. Then I drove back there, and she was coming out of the water . . ."

The pastor's voice softened and fell silent, and I could not persuade him to describe any more of what he had seen.

"Of course we all thought that poor Evvy had gone crazy," her mother said. "Turned out to be crazy like a fox." She said this without any hint of a smile.

I asked more questions, but neither of them said anything else beyond what I had already learned. So the three of us relaxed in lawn chairs in the front yard of the Amazing Evelyn's house, waiting for her to arrive from California for a promised visit. The grass was dry and brown. The vanes of the windmill turned with rasps and squeaks. I sipped lemonade and believed that I had managed to develop a sincere kinship with the

Amazing Evelyn's mother and pastor. After all, I had made it clear that I would not paint her as an object of amusement, as television did. It was my hope that their trust would convince Evelyn to trust me as well.

But then the telephone in the house rang, and the Amazing Evelyn's mother went to answer it. When she returned, she told me that Evelyn would not be coming home for a visit after all. She had heard that a journalist was lying in wait for her.

Those were her words: "lying in wait." As if I were a wild animal, hoping to devour her.

And as I watch her ascend, I wonder if she might have been right. My heart is racing, and the sensation in my belly has overtones of both hunger and sex. I do not want to watch her do this thing; I do not want to watch the Amazing Evelyn burn. And yet I watch anyway, as will thirty thousand people here tomorrow, as will millions more via television, as will you all.

She climbs the tower, never looking anywhere but upward, never acknowledging the existence of those of us below. She climbs until she is above the lights and we cannot see her except as a blue shadow in the darkness.

There is a movement beside me, and I am distracted for a moment. I glance to my right and see one of the Amazing Evelyn's assistants training a VHS camcorder upward. The other assistant stands beside her, head tilted back, gazing at the apex of the tower with an expression of beatific awe. She is in love with the Amazing Evelyn.

I look back up just in time. The blue shadow steps onto the platform and stands over the flame.

The flame leaps up, engulfing the shadow, and the Amazing Evelyn burns. She raises her arms, forming a fiery cross for an instant, and then dives. The sound is a roar; it is the sound of the wind rushing faster and faster, blasting all other sound behind, into the past, into oblivion.

She falls and burns forever. If her clothes are impregnated

with anything, it is gasoline. Her head is the amber coma of a comet; her torso a blazing blue spike; her arms and legs orange flames. Halfway through the fall the silver cape explodes, and there is no longer even a hint of head, of torso, of arms, of legs. The Amazing Evelyn is not a woman; she is fire. She is a falling star, a rushing meteor, spearing downward to crush me, to consume me —

I cry out, cringe, and hide my face in my hands.

Then I hear a splash and a sizzle, and drops of water spatter on my neck. The water is hot.

I straighten, uncover my eyes, and stare at the wet ash on my sleeve. Then, slowly, unwillingly, I turn to face the tank. I have a question to ask, the one question that my editor insisted I must ask despite its obvious, pathetic triteness. And ask it I shall; but I have waited until the moment when I know she will be most vulnerable, until the moment when I know that I have some hope of obtaining an answer that is honest, that is true.

The first word leaves my mouth as I turn:

"Why —" I begin, and then I stop.

Her assistants are in the tank, going to her with the robe, just as they will tomorrow. But tonight she waves them away, swims to the ladder, and rises from the water without their help, without the robe. She stands on the top step, at the rim of the tank, and looks down upon me. Her scent is sweet and terrifying.

Her tights and cape are gone, and her swimsuit is a blackened rag over her right shoulder. She is hairless; she is blistered; she is perfect.

Her assistants come up behind her. There is a hush in the arena, as if no one breathes. The Amazing Evelyn looks down upon me, her skin steaming, her eyes glowing.

"Did you get a good tape?" she asks. She is not speaking to me, but to her assistants.

"I think so," the assistant who held the camcorder says.

The Amazing Evelyn nods. "Then you may send it to

Zachary."

She descends the outer ladder to the floor, her eyes still on me. She knows that I too am in love with her.

Now she accepts the wet robe, puts it on, and turns to walk back across the arena to the illuminated door. Her assistants remain behind, as do I.

When she is gone, I touch the surface of the water in the tank again. It is warm. My finger comes up with a charred silver spangle, which I press to my lips. The assistants see me do this, but say nothing. They realize that I have finally understood: The Amazing Evelyn is indeed a conflagration artist; for when she burns, all who see her — who do not gawk, but *see* — burn with her.

"Why do you do it?" I was supposed to ask.

But having stood below her tower and watched her fall toward me, blazing through the black air of an empty arena, I know that the answer is as obvious as the question. She does it because it is her art.

She does it because it is her life.

Acknowledgments

The author would like to thank Edward L. Ferman of *The Magazine of Fantasy and Science Fiction* and Gardner Dozois of *Isaac Asimov's Science Fiction Magazine* for reasons to be found on the copyright page.

The author would also like to thank John and Kim Betancourt of The Wildside Press.

I am indebted to Steven Gould for his pithy and perceptive Introduction, Douglas Potter for his masterful illustrations, and Earl Cooley for heroic textfile conversions.

I am also indebted to my family and to far more friends than I can name for their encouragement and love. I hope you all know who you are.

Especially you, Barb.

— Bradley Denton
Austin, Texas
October 1991